America Deceived II

America Deceived II

Homeland Security Warning:
Possession of this novel may result
in enhanced interrogation.

E.A. Blayre III

iUniverse, Inc.
New York Bloomington

America Deceived II
Homeland Security Warning: Possession of this novel may result in enhanced interrogation.

This is a work of fiction. All of the characters, names, incidents, organizations, and dialogue in this novel are either the products of the author's imagination or are used fictitiously.

iUniverse books may be ordered through booksellers or by contacting:

iUniverse
1663 Liberty Drive
Bloomington, IN 47403
www.iuniverse.com
1-800-Authors (1-800-288-4677)

ISBN: 978-1-4502-5743-5 (pbk)
ISBN: 978-1-4502-5744-2 (ebk)

Printed in the United States of America

iUniverse rev. date: 9/22/10

CHAPTER I

Christmas Day - 2021

General Barker flipped open the hardcover manual, scanned location sites and hand checked each coordinate, "They launched it."

"Are you sure?"

"Affirmed."

President Jack Fremont III slid further down into his chair.

"Anyone determine an exact point of origin?"

General Barker shook his head and looked at the computer technician holding up his index and middle finger.

"Point of origin in two minutes, Mr. President."

The President pulled an antique timepiece from his vest pocket and watched as ornate hands slowly circled the gold faceplate. General Barker inhaled his cigarette, in a single breath, down to the stained yellow filter.

Satellite graphs lines converged on a map point in the Middle East area of the globe.

"Point of origin established sir."

"Give it to me."

"Israel. City of Dimona, Israel."

Silence spread across the room, even the computers quieted down.

ABC news reporter Amy Milford, in town to compose an editorial puff-piece for the administration, hastily wrote short-hand notes on her yellow legal pad.

President Fremont glanced over, "This is off-the-record."

She stopped writing, clutched the notepad under her arm and blended into the background.

"I know."

The President wheeled around behind his mahogany desk, "This is going to be a PR nightmare."

He tucked the watch back into his vest and asked, "Which Arab neighbor receives her belated Chanukah surprise?"

"Saudi Arabia, Syria, Lebanon."

"Probably Iran."

Inferior officers constantly passed him updated, detailed satellite pictures of the launch site releasing the warhead.

General Barker studied the snapshots, his numerous medals clanged together as he quickly scribbled equations, then held the pictures up to the recessed, overhead track lighting. He tilted his face slightly and removed his cap, "It appears to be a long range missile."

"Long range?"

General Barker re-examined several satellite photos, double-checked his math and handed it to the President, "Check out the design, size and markings."

"Not wasting a long range on a neighbor, that eliminates the entire Middle East. Punch up a map where this damn thing can cause damage."

General Barker rubbed his baldhead, "Basically, anywhere on Earth."

The President yelled to his Secretary of State, "Get someone on the phone from Israel, pronto."

General Barker examined another series of enhanced photos as they rolled out of the satellite color printer, "Where's the impact zone?"

The President shifted in his seat, "I don't need this today."

The satellite technician raised his arm with all fingers out-stretched, "Delineating point of impact in five minutes."

Reporter Amy Milford jotted down another series of notes on her palm.

President Fremont glared at her then turned to General Barker, "I bet Russia pissed them off with their steadfast support of those bomb-happy Arabs."

General Barker smoked another cigarette, "Israel would never attack the Soviet Union. They possess nearly as many warheads as us. They'd be committing suicide out of fear of death."

President Fremont planted his hands on the desk and lifted himself from his chair.

"Did anybody call them yet?"

An officer held up the phone, "On hold."

"Tell him he has ten seconds to pick up."

General Barker patted the President on the back, "Relax. We'll deal with this. Israel is our ally."

"I am speaking to him right now, Mr. President."

President Fremont grabbed the phone, "What in God's name are you doing over there?"

The President yelled for a few moments then slammed down the receiver.

"Bastards denied the launch. They're trying to convince me that our satellites are picking up a military training exercise. They said that they detected a missile launch from Karachi, Pakistan."

Another inferior officer spread a color fax across the desk, "Here, Israel HQ just sent this Intel showing a Karachi launch site. Maybe, it did launch from Pakistan. "

"Bullshit, call again. Tell him I'm holding our satellite photographs in my hand."

"Will do."

The satellite technician interrupted, "Mapping coordinates, destination in three minutes."

ABC news reporter Amy Milford clicked on her pocket voice recorder.

President Fremont stared out the regal bay window, watching heavy snowflakes bury the White House grounds.

"China, what about China, Bark?"

Only the President called him 'Bark', all the ladies referred to him in whispers as General Barker, our beloved 'four-star rapist'.

The General shook his head, "For what reason?"

"De-stabilizing banks, tanking fiat currency..."

"Too risky."

He paced around the room, "We should discuss this more privately."

General Barker dismissed non-essential members of the military contingent and overtook total control of satellite GPS mapping.

"Computer's still simulating missile track. At least a few more minutes till we acquire point of impact."

President Fremont casually strode over to the reporter and stuck his hand into her breast pocket. He removed the tape recorder while whispering in her ear, "No more recording or note-taking, these men," he pointed with his eyes toward the Secret Service, "...these men are deadly serious."

The President smiled at his paramour and nonchalantly slipped the listening device into his pocket. He faced the group and said, "North Korea then."

"They'd have cover for them. That's better than 50/50."

A bright, red phone rang and rang until General Barker snatched up the headset. He cupped it against his ear and nodded to voices on the other side.

"That was our inside guy. Secondary confirmation on Dimona as the launch site. Israel fired the nuke alright."

President Fremont asked, "Does he know the destination?"

"Negative. Top secret."

"I don't need this on Christmas. My family's waiting. I scheduled photo-ops all over town, tonight and tomorrow."

"I'm sure their reasoning is sound. As soon as we know the intended target, we'll wrap this up and enjoy the holiday."

The reporter adjusted her bra strap, triggering a recording wire embedded in her brassiere cup. She'd be damned she'd miss the biggest story of her 'casting couch' career. Lover or not, this rose to Nobel Prize territory.

She slyly positioned herself behind the General to record his announcement. President Fremont closed his eyes tightly. A Secret Service officer crept up behind her.

President Fremont mouthed, "I'm sorry."

An officer jammed a sharpened metal awl through the back of her throat. She gurgled and tumbled over. Her notepad dropped from her grip and lodged beneath her neck as she collapsed to the floor. Her last words, written on her favorite notepad, in her own blood.

General Barker directed the clean-up, "If she's still alive, bring her to my office and leave her there. Otherwise, dump her by that Senator she used to date."

"Check."

The Secret Service confiscated the legal pad, tape machines and brassiere recorder then dragged her draining body out, palms down. Another detail scrubbed the room.

Flashing lights pulsated across the monitor. Graph lines calculated the height, speed and estimated fuel of the missile, tracking it on the computer generated geographic map, running from Dimona, Israel to the destination site.

"Location, confirmed."

President Fremont sat on top of the desk and asked, "So, who's unwrapping this Christmas day gift?"

General Barker eyes widened as he stared at the computer screen. He swivelled it away, lit up another Lucky Strike tobacco and sat down.

President Fremont walked over to him, close enough to inhale second-hand smoke and gestured to the room.

"Don't leave us in suspense, where's it hitting Bark?"

He took a long drag, "Washington, D.C., time to evacuate, Mr. President."

Near the Senator's offices in the Russell building, police detained a man leaving the area where a slender woman's body laid.

Detective Warren Nash and Patrolman James 'BlackJack' Jones moved in and secured the scene, regulating arriving police officers to crowd control and decorating the area with yellow 'Do Not Cross' streamers.

"Any I.D. on her?"

BlackJack rifled through her pockets.

"Nothing, she seems familiar though."

Her angelic face and platinum blonde hair remained undisturbed. A pencil-sized hole in her neck bled slowly as the area coagulated. Drag marks from her stiletto heels led away from the capitol building.

Detective Nash gestured toward the patrol car.

"Who's the guy in the paddy wagon?"

"Don't know yet, not even sure he's involved."

"Where did you find him?"

"About a block away on foot."

They turned their attention back to the stiffening woman with her back pressed to the ground and shirt buttoned disjointedly.

Her waxy skin turned purple. Her lips, finger and toe nails faded to pale colors as blood drained away and pooled in her lower abdomen causing a dark purple-black lividity. Her hands and feet turned blue as both eyes sunk into her skull.

Detective Nash lifted her shirt with the end of his pen.

"Someone ripped off her bra."

"Sexual assault then?"

"Possibly."

He circled the body.

"Start with the basics, we must find out who she is...check that, who she was."

"No purse, no I.D."

"Call dispatch, inquire about missing persons. Girl this attractive does not go missing unnoticed."

"Unless she's a prostitute."

Detective Nash shook his head, "She's not a prostitute."

"Look at the bruising on her arms."

"Those are fresh bruises, not whore bruises."

A voice from the shadows blurted, "I knows who that is."

Detective Nash commanded, “Come over here.” He pointed to the corpse on the ground, “You know this lady?”

The homeless man emerged from the building’s shade, “I’s do.”

“How do you know her, you kill her?”

He clutched his stained wool cap, “No, sir.”

Detective Nash grabbed him by his arm, “How do you know her?”

“She’s Amy Milford from the newscast, ABC, I think. We watch her all the time in the shelter.”

“I think that’s her.”

Detective Nash pulled BlackJack aside, “Bring me a photo of her. We’re not going to start identifying victims from bums on the street.”

He returned to the disheveled man.

“Thanks for your assistance,” said Detective Nash as he escorted the homeless man into a police cruiser for later questioning. As he pushed the bum in, he pulled out a man handcuffed the gentlemen’s way and leaned him on the front hood of the patrol car.

“What’s your name?”

“Jason Schwartz.”

“Mr. Schwartz, I feel like I know you. Have we crossed paths before?”

“I don’t think so.”

Detective Nash frisked him and asked, “Jason, my new friend, what were you doing so close to that dead body?”

“I never even saw her. I was jogging on the bike path, over there by the woods.” He pulled up his fleece winter jacket, “See the sweat suit.”

“Am I to believe that you’re out jogging on this cold, snowy day? I guess nobody invited you for Christmas dinner.”

“You figured it out. Perhaps, Schwartz gave it away.” He paused and added, “Detective.”

“Don’t get wise Schwartz, you’ll spend Christmas in jail.”

Jason smiled, “Better than in church.”

Detective Nash pushed him into the hood, “Wrong thing to say today.”

“I’m sorry. I joke around when I’m nervous. I apologize. Just an anxious habit, my stupid comments.”

Detective Nash picked him up, “Alright, let’s start over. You have I.D?”

“Sure.”

He reached with both cuffed hands into his pocket and produced a license and identification cards.

“What’s all that?”

“Driver’s license.”

"No, all those other cards."

"PBA badge, Detective card, Honorary FBI card and others from various prominent public officials." He fanned them out on the hood of the patrol car and picked one up, "Here's one signed by the President."

Detective Nash gathered up the license and cards.

"Stay right here."

He held up his handcuffed wrists, "I'm not going anywhere."

Detective Nash jumped into the seat of his patrol car, entered his access code and punched the name and license into the computer. Everything came back squeaky clean, not even a traffic infraction.

He walked over while reading the identification out loud, "Jason Schwartz, you have a lot of friends in high places."

"Now that you've verified them, can I be on my way?"

Detective Nash threw each card, one-by-one, while repeating, "Not gonna help...Not gonna help...Not gonna help..."

Detective Nash opened the police car door, and forcibly sat Jason in the back seat.

"We'll talk later at the precinct, Mr. Schwartz. Christmas Day and you even got your wish."

He slammed the door shut behind him.

Detective Nash left the patrol car locked and re-entered the crime scene by ducking under yellow tape as back-up police officers cordoned off the entire area, draping streamers from branch to branch to branch.

"Enough with the yellow ribbon, guys. You're not decorating your goddamn Christmas tree."

A police officer from a dense part of the woods yelled back, "I wish I was," to the delight of the squad.

BlackJack returned from the mobile Crime Scene Unit van holding a photo of the news-reporter.

"Sure looks like her."

Detective Nash snatched the picture and compared it to the body, "You're right. Let's be certain and do a quick fingerprint identification."

He tossed a digital camera to BlackJack.

"Photograph her before you print her."

BlackJack snapped photos then scraped caked-on mud from her hands with a wooden tongue depressor.

"Something's written on her palm."

Detective Nash looked over, even his dyslexia failed to stop him from reading the scrawled message, "Israel did it."

He repeated, "Israel did it, Israel did it, what the hell does that mean?"

Clouds dissolved, haze reddened the setting sunshine, yanking the sun away from Earth as daylight grew brighter and brighter, resembling early morning than late afternoon. Time not simply froze but reversed, night turned into day, dark became light, pm turned am, days, months and years lost meaning.

Ear drum piercing explosions followed by loud rumbling burst forth, criss-crossing the sky, bright, intense lights blinded all seeing beings, tornados of compressed air funneled to a sharp point, dancing on the ground. Dense pitch-dark rain blotted out the brightness. Ground tremors rolled up flat-lands into small hills. Wave after wave of splitting atoms raced across the land. Wind gusts ravaged standing structures, blowing with olympian force, generating wind lines visible to the naked eye.

Detective Nash awakened to dead silence. Blood steadily flowed from his ears, nose, mouth and eyes. Stumps of trees, stalks of flowers and singed grass, dotted the barren land. Manufactured snowfalls covered the unholy mess. Outlines of people turned to dust beneath the heavy, noxious snow. Naked men, women and children with skin hanging off their arms, pock holes in their face and clumped, crisp, patches of hair, wandered the streets, mute, like sick dogs circling for suitable places to die.

He closed his eyes and joined them.

CHAPTER II

20 Years Earlier, *September 11, 2001*
corner of Vesey Street and Washington, New York City
Inside World Trade Center Building #7, 23rd Floor

The CIA agent hung up the phone.

General Barker noticed his sly smile and asked, "Who was that?"

"Ted."

"What did he want?"

"He asked if that cheating bitch boarded the plane."

General Barker laughed, "Did you tell him we escorted Barbara to Flight 77, over an hour ago?"

"That's exactly what I said."

"Alright, time for serious business then."

"One and Two are set, ready to go. This building is on standby. Planes go airborne in about an hour."

"And the evidence?"

"Dropped shithead's passport near the towers in a place where even the NYPD can find it. Our Mossad friends parked the car at Logan this morning with their luggage."

"What did you put inside the bags?"

"Koran, videocassettes from a Boeing 767 Flight Simulator, training manuals and a couple martyr tapes. Mossad tossed in a suicide note naming each hijacker."

"Everything's in place then. Grab some popcorn and wait for the show to start."

The CIA agent sat down checking his notes. General Barker hovered over the desk, reviewing various mock exercises planned for the day. The CIA agent's cell phone rang.

A garbled, double-coded voice on the other end spoke, "Employees of Odigo just received e-mails warning people to stay away from the World Trade Center complex."

He shook his head, "Yesterday, the stock trades and today this. We haven't even lifted the curtain and we're in trouble."

The encrypted voice said, "Over-riding their computer notification system now. That's the last message transmitted."

The CIA agent hung up, "Not good, not good. Too many people involved. Too many competing interests. Too many variables."

General Barker barely responded as he concentrated on numerous training missions developed by Pentagon Brass to insert phantom airliners, disable NORAD and confuse Air Traffic Controllers. He ordered fighter jets flown away from New York City and Washington D.C.

On a busy day at the Windows on the World restaurant, one-hundred-and-seven floors above ground in the North tower, the owner's favorite waitress set the breakfast table for her daily patron.

The crimson-jacketed, stuffy concierge grabbed the server by her hand, "Stop setting this table, Larry's not coming today."

She jerked her arm away, "Are you sure? He hasn't missed morning breakfast since he bought this place."

"I know. To be honest I thought it was a prank. I nearly called his wife out on it."

She started setting the place again, "He sits here every day."

"Not today."

"I don't believe you. He's coming and you'll thank me for saving both our jobs."

"I'm telling you, I just spoke to his wife."

The dressed-up, white trash waitress swept beneath the table, dusted surfaces and wiped off each chair.

"I'm setting him a spot."

"His wife called, he's sick. He's not coming."

"I still do not believe you."

The over-paid, over-tipped waitress snapped her gum and continued to neatly arrange place-mats, forks, spoons and knives. She set a pint of Orange Juice, which she freshly squeezed, on the centerpiece of the table and folded cloth napkins into swans. Larry always remarked that she reminded him of the beauty and grace of a swan. Sometimes, it was the lone thing that brightened her day. Larry went out-of-his-way to ask about her out-of-wedlock children. He even gave them gifts for their birthdays.

"Mr. Silverstein will be in, I know it."

The uptight concierge shook his head, "You're wasting your time."

"Sorry, but I know him. Only the devil himself could keep him from being here."

"Fine, but when you're done wait on tables with actual customers."

The snot-nosed concierge returned to his post, checked in diners and escorted guests to tables. An undocumented alien, filling chef jobs Americans do not want, snuck around from the rear kitchen, tapped the waitress on her shoulder and whispered, "I agree with you. Mister Silverstein will be here."

"I know."

The waitress winked and smiled as she finished preparing the table and readied for her favorite part of the day.

A live video feed from the nose camera of Flight #11 turned on, multiple High Definition television screens inside the President's bulletproof limousine lit up with images of the American Airlines Boeing 767 whipping through noisy winds, drawing the box-like skyline of New York City, closer and closer.

The operation, known among bacchanalian circles as 'The Big Wedding', kicked off with a bang...

Employees of Urban Moving Systems parked the white van in Liberty park, New Jersey, a perfect back-drop of the World Trade Center. They removed their Saudi Arabian style robes and carefully unwound dark turbans into the passenger seat.

"Grab the Nikon."

Jason Schwartz snagged his camera by the strap, looked through the viewfinder and framed an artful shot of the steel twins.

"Tower One is on the right, focus on it first."

"We're going in numerical order then?"

He laughed as he zoomed in to the colossal exoskeletal structures, glimmering brightly in a cloudless blue sky.

"My turn, start filming."

One of the other employees jumped before the camera and danced like a cracker at a hip hop club. They all laughed.

"I'm next."

Another UMS worker mocked his partner's dance then flicked a Bic® lighter several times close to the camera and in the foreground of the Twin Towers.

Jason waved them away from the viewfinder, "Enough fooling around, it's just about time."

He checked his gold Rolex wristwatch, a gift from his Mossad handlers, and synchronized the clock, 8:46:26 a.m...

American Airlines Flight #11 roared over an innocent city at breakneck speeds and sliced on an angle through the silver North Tower between the 94th and 98th floors. New York trembled as Tower One enveloped the plane like a pesky horsefly caught and cocooned in a spider's glistening web.

"Hit the plunger."

General Barker pressed the red button.

Freight elevators, stationed near underground support columns, exploded. Trapped energy tore up through the basement levels, demolishing chunks of the main lobby area as prominent, thick marble tiling dislodged from walls and crashed to the floor, shattering into jagged pieces.

The earpiece transponder commanded, "Hold steady, the next plane incoming, e.t.a. 15 minutes."

Back in New Jersey...

"Holy shit. Did you get that on film?"

"I did. It was better than I thought."

UMS employees broke into another dance. An elderly lady watched from her bedroom window while dialing the police.

Inside the adjacent tower, cubical office workers, security personnel, cleaning ladies, secretaries, maintenance men, janitors, assistants, and bellhops pried their faces away from the windows, lined up and started marching orderly down stairs, assisting the handicapped and lifting the feeble as they evacuated the South Tower.

The South Tower Public Address system blared several times and announced, "Do not evacuate. Fires in the North Tower are under control. Remain in the South Tower as there may be falling debris outside. Please return to your offices."

People looked up at the anonymous voice emanating from dimpled metal boxes and kept walking. The trusting ones turned around and returned to their high rise offices.

One of the trusting ones, while walking back upstairs, thought about the evacuees, '*Fools, hope a steel beam drops on your heads.*'

The South Tower PA system blared and announced again, "Do not evacuate, return to your offices at once. This is for your own safety. Fires in the North Tower are under control. The South Tower is not in danger."

Just as the trusting one sat at his desk on the 80th floor, he glanced at the walnut clock his daughter gave him, 9:02:54 a.m...

United Airlines Flight 175 disappeared like a cartoon-cutout, swallowed whole by the South Tower, between the 78th and 84th floors. Enormous titanium airplane engines tore from their wings, sailed through offices, bathrooms, gyms, doors, hallways, safes, beams, walls, kitchens and crashed to the street, blocks away. Office paper birds flew out of the gaping hole and gently floated to the ground carrying names of the dead.

On the clearest day of the year, New York City clouded up.

Nestled snugly inside the Emma E. Booker Elementary schoolhouse in Sarasota Florida, the President of the United States kept reading the mesmerizing, magical book to the second grade class, "... 'Yes,' her dad said. 'That goat saved my car.'..."

As per the script, Andy Card entered the room from stage left and delivered his lines.

"We are under attack."

The President raised his eyebrows, turned the page and continued, "... The car robber said, 'something hit me when I was trying to steal that car'. The girl said, 'My goat hit you'..."

CNN interrupted the President's Book Club and broadcasted footage of Palestinians celebrating Saddam Hussein's 1991 invasion of Kuwait with the headline, 'Palestinians celebrate 9/11.' Reuters and AP picked up the news and plastered it across the World.

Behind the hardened area of the Pentagon, a board meeting took place...

"Does everyone have their laptops? Open up the section regarding the Pentagon's Budget. Use your installed hardware, internet's down again."

A century-old civilian accountant raised his hand, "I was just over in D.O.D. and the internet's running fine over there. Perhaps you should check it again."

The Pentagon's Budget Analyst tried to connect his computer.

"No dice, no signal. Without further interruptions, scroll down the page to a folder labeled Department of Defense spending, fiscal years 1999-2001. That is where we were told to search."

"Search for what," asked a lifelong bookkeeper who sat on a folding chair in the corner of the room.

"Missing money, a whole shit load of it."

The medal-less Pentagon employees laughed. They asked all at once, "How much is a shit load?"

"2.3 trillion. Obviously none of you watched C-Span yesterday as I instructed."

Civilian workers of Resource Services Washington sheepishly looked to the ground, a few laughed.

"I'll fill you in. Secretary of Defense Donald Rumsfeld testified on Capital Hill yesterday and he talked about money missing from the Pentagon's budget. Over two trillion dollars."

"And…"

"And he called me yesterday. First time in my career, he called personally. He instructed me to schedule this early meeting and said that it is the task of everyone in this room to find it. Find the trillions. His exact words."

A quota-hired receptionist creaked open the door and slid into a seat in the back row. The Senior Budget Analyst snapped, "You're late."

"Sorry, it's just that as I was arriving, I heard on the radio that a plane hit the World Trade Center. Possibly even two planes."

He grabbed a remote and pressed the power button, the wall-mounted television flickered.

"Tv's out too. No Internet, busy phones and no television. This is a real first rate outfit we're running here."

He clicked off the television and said, "Let's get back to business, Secretary Rumsfeld told me these trillions of dollars missing from the Pentagon budget are our number one priority."

Deep below multiple levels of heavy metal blast doors, bolted inside the cold, steel White House bunker, the Vice-President slithered into his tall black leather chair, gnawing on Beef Jerky. He sat hunched, more like coiled, in a corner. Saliva pooled in his mouth. Scotch was the order of the day. Nobody does this sober.

Transportation Secretary Norman Mineta ninja-ed through the meddlesome security. They attempted to stop him at every checkpoint. He joined the Vice-President in the bunker. As the Asian samurai sat, the door opened behind him. A young man, some 3rd generation General's son, leaned in and said, "Airplane is fifty miles out, Mr. Vice-President, sir."

"Private, what are you doing back here again?"

"It's just that plane..."

"Follow my orders."

"It's heading right for..."

"Leave here immediately and learn to follow orders. I am in command."

He hurried off and left the Vice President and the Secretary of Transportation alone.

"We need to stop that plane, Dick."

The Vice President shook his head.

The wise man's mind could not comprehend what his thinned eyes told him. He sat quietly and started opening them wider and wider. He privately contemplated the meaning of treason. He remembered learning in grade school about Benedict Arnold handing over the fort named after him, Fort Arnold, to the British. This was not like that at all...or was it? He occupied his time by defining it in different manners to himself as he watched, then re-defined and watched more.

Doors flew open frantically. Another young soldier scrambled inside.

"10 miles out, sir. Do the orders still stand?"

Scales on the Vice President's neck overlapped as he whipped around and yelled, "Of course the orders still stand, have you heard anything to the contrary!?"

Officially, the Pentagon Budget Analysts Meeting involuntarily adjourned, without resolution, permanently, at 9:37:26 a.m.

Back in New York City, CIA agents and General Barker eavesdropped on firefighter's radio transmissions as they rushed into the South Tower.

Ladder 15 headquarters radioed on the scratchy out-dated equipment, "Battalion Fifteen to Battalion Seven."

"Go Ladder 15."

"What do you got up there, Chief?"

"I'm still in boy stair 74th floor. No smoke or fire problems, walls are breached, so be careful."

"Yeah Ten-Four, I saw that on 68. Alright, we're on 71 we're coming up behind you."

"Ten-four. Six more to go."

"Let me know when you see more fire."

"I found a Marshall on 75."

The CIA agent rested his headphones on the table.

"How did they reach the 75th floor already?"

General Barker shook his head, "No idea. That cannot be right. Patch it through speakerphone."

The CIA agent switched the firefighter radio transmissions to speakerphone.

He heard Chief Palmer, a physical specimen that rushed up staircases two-steps at a time carrying hundreds of pounds of equipment and the weight of New York City on his back, communicate from the impact sight.

He looked out the gaping hole with steel bent inward, wind ripped through his soul as he counted dead body after dead body.

"Numerous 10-45's, Code Ones."

Chief Palmer searched for survivors and assessed the situation.

"Battalion Seven ... Ladder 15, we've got two isolated pockets of fire. We should be able to knock it down with two lines. Radio that, 78th floor numerous 10-45 Code Ones."

He needed to add many more casualties, present company included.

The CIA agent shut off the speakerphone. He spoke on a secure line to the White House bunker.

"Remove all firefighters, evacuate both towers and enter the final phase."

General Barker snatched the headset from him, "No time. The NYFD moved too quickly, we must pull it down now."

The CIA agent wrestled it back, "No way. We're supposed to run this with as little collateral damage as possible. I'm issuing a Code Red and removing the firefighters."

General Barker grabbed the main feed from headquarters while pushing the agent into the wall.

"Get him out of here."

Military guards removed the CIA agent.

General Barker communicated through the scrambled line, "Nobody leaves the towers. Jam all radio transmissions. Start the countdown."

Across the river from New York, in ugly step-child New Jersey...

"You see that, you see that."

Jason panned across the smoldering towers. He stopped dancing and stared at the other men jumping and slapping high-fives. They didn't notice his smile fade away. He saw the native's eyes darting through opening and closing curtains, sharpening in on him and his friends as they celebrated.

New Jersey authorities dispatched police cars to Liberty Park after receiving reports of possible collaborators.

Jason warned his fellow agents, "Take it easy on the celebrating, people are watching."

"This is a great day, my friend. For us and our country."

Jason dismantled the equipment, "Time to go, party's over." He looked over his shoulder, "Did anyone just hear those sirens?"

His friend opened his arms and gestured to the sky, "Sirens are everywhere, my friend. It is a song for our future."

"Take it easy. We filmed it, we should go."

The group broke into a chorus..."New York, New York, the city so nice, we hit it twice."

New Jersey's finest, Detective Warren Nash and patrolman James 'BlackJack' Jones coasted around the back of the park, sirens silent and snuck up on the celebrants.

Detective Nash jumped from behind the concrete wall in a shooter's stance, held out his revolver and said, "Hold it right there."

He directed with his weapon, "You with the camera, walk slowly over to your friends."

Several agents huddled together.

"Frisk them, I'll keep them honest."

BlackJack patted down each man, removed a few box cutters and handed them to the detective.

"Cuff these guys then search their car. With all this shit breaking down today, do an explosive test."

BlackJack slapped metal handcuffs on the muscular guys and plastic zip ties on the weaker, then headed off to their van.

Minutes later he yelled up, "K-9's getting positive hits for traces of explosives."

Detective Nash pressed his handgun to the temple of Jason's head, "You're involved then."

"We are not your problems, they, the Palestinians are your problems."

Detective Nash knocked him to the floor and contacted headquarters.

"Dispatch."

"Nash and BlackJack Jones, requesting back-up, Liberty Park, New Jersey. Five possible suspects."

"Gotcha, back-up on the way, stat. Log in their names and time of arrest."

Detective Nash muttered, "Endless computer paperwork."

He punched in the detainees' names then logged the time into the police cruiser's on-board computer, 9:59:04 a.m...

Liquid molten metal poured down the skeletal facing then rumbling explosions traveled up and down the South tower causing it to drop at free-fall speed as it mushroomed to the ground. Half-hour later, the twin sibling fell the same way.

Dark clouds higher than the once-dwarfed remaining skyscrapers, raced down alleyways, tore through streets, blew out windows, wobbled store fronts, crushed fire trucks and buried cars, carrying desks, legs, chairs, arms, laptops, laps, file cabinets, torsos, computers, skulls, televisions, eyes, cell-phones, ears, pulverized cement and paper across lower Manhattan.

God waited an eternity, piously swept away the debris and pulled back the shade ... New York's beating heart, gone forever.

The President read and read and read and read, "...The girl hugged the goat. Her Dad said, 'The goat can stay with us. And he can eat all the cans and canes and caps and capes he wants.'..."

He closed the book.

The powers-that-be waited until the world panicked, loudly re-broadcasted the spellbinding event all day, invented the hypnotizing television crawl notification system, blamed nineteen cave-dwelling Arabs and quietly pulled down World Trade Center, Building #7 during dinner.

Gotham's Mayor waited a week then hastily deployed mammoth-sized cranes to rapidly cart away smoking nano-thermite covered steel intermixed with NYFD body parts, on barges, to the Fresh Kills landfill before being sold at yard sale prices to China.

Mission Accomplished, Operation Big Wedding.

CHAPTER III

Present Day, New Year's Eve, 2021...

Detective Nash started to wake up...he pointed at the male nurse.

"I recognize you...I recognize you...Jason..."

The male nurse hurried off passing by BlackJack as he walked into the room and sat on a chair next to the bed.

"First one here on visiting hours."

He stared over the gurney into his face.

"You awake, buddy?"

He shook him.

"Happy New Year"

Detective Nash rolled over, "Yeah, not quite yet." He felt the dressings tightly squeezed around his entire body. "What happened back there?"

BlackJack pulled the medical chart off the end of the hospital bed, flipped through a few pages and said, "You don't want to know."

"Tell me."

"I'll tell you when you're in better shape and have the time."

Detective Nash pointed with his wrapped hands toward the IV's, heart monitors and blood pressure machine confining him to the bed.

"Nothing but time"

BlackJack hung the chart on a hook, "Rest now. We'll talk tomorrow."

"I remember investigating a girl's murder..."

"Later, later."

Headaches sledge-hammered his brain while his memory erupted, "... then we arrested a homeless guy and another guy...Jewish guy jogging..."

"Rest, my friend."

Pounding and pulsating pains reverberated through his brain, "... murder of a girl, an ABC news-reporter. Help me, help me with the pieces I'm missing."

"I don't think you're ready for it."

He popped aspirins into his mouth and took a swig of water, "I'm ready."

BlackJack leaned over and spoke softly into his reconstructed ear, "You remember what happened to Chief Finnigan on September 10, 2001?"

"Of course I remember. A punk kid shot him that day."

He opened his coat, "Right here, missed his heart by a few inches."

"I remember, no one in the force saw him for weeks. Weren't even allowed to visit him in the hospital."

"Doctors pronounced Chief dead more than a dozen times. Next few days, he remained in a coma, undisturbed. Similar to the coma you experienced these last few weeks."

"You're not doing a very good job of cheering me up."

"Let me finish the point. For reasons never understood by medical science, one day Chief's eyes opened. He expected teams of doctors and nurses marveling at his awakening. Instead, he woke up to an entire hospital staff walking around like Zombies. Real 'night-of-the-living-dead' type shit. Entire place looked like hell, pure hell. Didn't see a smile for the next week. Nobody told him a thing. Didn't even give him a television. Hospital staff told him it was for his own good. He finally found out what happened. Nobody could keep that secret forever, 9/11 and all. Doctors told him that shock from 9/11 would have jeopardized his recovery. Could've killed him."

"Doesn't mean they were right."

"According to Chief, they were right. When he found out about 9/11 days later, his heart ripped apart. He passed out, his blood pressure dropped and doctors feared for his life. That's when he knew they were right. Opening his eyes and being confronted by jets slamming into towers and murdering men from his precinct...would have been too much."

Detective Nash raised his arms, "What's that have to do with me?"

"I'll tell you what you need to know when the time is right. Now the time is not right, like it was not right for him then."

Detective Nash sat up in the bed, "I can take it."

"Not tonight, tomorrow's visiting hours, I promise."

BlackJack walked to the door. Detective Nash summoned all his strength and yelled, "You walk out that door and we're through as partners."

BlackJack turned around and smiled, "You know, you say that once a day."

"It works."

BlackJack returned to the fake leather recliner seat positioned next to the bed, "It's losing effectiveness."

Detective Nash laid back down and asked, "So, what happened?"

"We were attacked."

"We? You mean, you and me?"

"You, me and the country."

Detective Nash propped himself up on his elbows, "America, someone attacked America?"

"We barely averted our Hiroshima."

"Nuclear?"

BlackJack nodded.

"Who?"

"Pakistan. Crazy f'n Arabs."

Detective Nash closed his eyes and settled into his rigid hospital pillow, "Does this have anything to do with why I am in here?"

BlackJack crossed his hands, "DOD intercepted the warhead with a Patriot missile. They blew it up in the atmosphere, greatly lessening the impact. It still reached the ground with force but not enough to wipe out the city."

"Am I full of toxic radiation?"

"Do you have any super powers?"

Detective Nash cracked a grin, "I used my x-ray vision on that blonde nurse."

"I spoke with your doctor, they tested you and you're within normal levels. Otherwise you'd be sleeping in a de-contamination unit."

"How did I survive?"

"Your doctors told me that paramedics found you behind a broken telephone pole. The light pole cracked inches over your head, shielding you from the blast. I don't buy it. I think your thick skull saved you."

"How'd you make it then, same affliction?"

"The black-and-white protected me. The squad car flipped over and over, tossed me around like a rag doll."

"Any other survivors?"

BlackJack looked down, "Just you and I."

"Nobody... not the other officers...not the homeless man... not the jogger?"

"All vaporized. It could have been worse. Thank God, Patriot missiles intercepted the nuke and saved thousands of lives."

Detective Nash shook his head, "Damn tragedy, what can I do to help?"

"Headquarters will not medically release you. They diverted all of our man-power undercover to root out sympathetic Arab terrorists. They say you're in no condition right now for undercover work. Desk only, that's straight from HQ."

"If I cannot help there, I'll work the case with that dead reporter."

"There's nothing left on that case. The girl's body turned to ash in the blast. No body, no crime."

Detective Nash raised his hand, "Her body, written on her body... I remember something written on her palm..."

"I don't remember that."

"... 'Israel did it'...written across her palm... 'Israel did it'..."

BlackJack shook his head, "No, no, no...no."

"There was something definitely written on her hand."

He shook quicker, "No...no...no...no..."

"I'm 100% certain, 'Israel did it.' right across the hand."

BlackJack grabbed his chin, "No...no...wait a minute...you're right. I remember, 'Israel did it' scrawled on her palm. We solved that part of the case."

"You solved it, how?"

"Writing on her palm, pointed to her killer. Dying declaration, is the legal term I believe."

"Dying declaration?"

"Yes, yes. 'Israel did it' referred to her killer, Dov Israel, the senior Senator from Florida."

Detective Nash sat straight up in the bed, "Dov killed her? Dov 'the Dove' Israel killed her? He's an anti-war peacenik. He rescues puppies from shelters. He builds houses for the homeless."

"Peacenik means nothing. Remember Ira Einhorn killed some chic and left her to rot in the closet. Holly Maddox or something like that. Nobody thought he did it. Heck, they even gave him his own special Earth Day."

He settled back down when the blood pressure monitor numbers increased, "I am aware of the Unicorn Killer. But Dov Israel, he works for PETA, nurses injured birds and saves whales, it does not add up."

"Apparently they carried on an affair."

"She wrote her killer's name on her palm...and it's him, Senator Israel. He's in his eighties, no way."

"Relax, we'll talk more when you gain your strength."

"An 80-year-old man stabbed a girl in the throat while carrying on an affair. Is that really the working theory in the department?"

"Case closed, we hear he's taking a plea."

"Not everyone who takes a plea did the crime."

"Rest and I'll give you the case file tomorrow."

Detective Nash turned over in the bed and closed his eyes, "Alright, just one more thing..."

BlackJack walked to the door, "Don't say it...Don't say it...not this New Year's Eve."

Detective Nash popped a few pain pills, "See you next year."

BlackJack left the trauma unit, passing by a male nurse. The orderly brought in a cold, gray plastic tray of portioned food. He positioned it on top of the pull-out table.

"When you're finished be sure to use your napkin."

Detective Nash buried his head in the pillow and thought to himself, *'Just my luck, a male nurse and a female doctor.'*

He gave up trying to sleep, opened the tray and choked down rubbery chicken, cold peas and rock solid bread. For $5,000-a-night, the hospital food managed to elevate McDonalds ® to edible. He finished the Unhappy Meal and wiped his partially wrapped face with a napkin. He pushed aside the tray and felt the bandages around his head.

'Let's see how I look"

He grabbed a mirror off the table and checked the dressings.

'A burqa showed more skin.'

Detective Nash noticed a dark smudge across his bandaged chin and rubbed it off.

"Ink."

He pulled over the metal garbage can, retrieved a discarded napkin and opened it.

He read the smeared message, 'I survived.'

Detective Nash grabbed an orderly's arm as she cleaned his bedpan, "What's the name of the male nurse that was just here?"

"I think you're mistaken."

"Tall guy, a nurse, I believe. He was just here."

"We do not have any male nurses on this floor."

Dr. Eugene Abrams opened curtains across the basement laboratory window. He pushed corrugated cardboard boxes to the center of a slate table. He grabbed the first box addressed from "Turin, Italy" and sliced it open with a razor sharp box-cutter. He sifted through filler materials then reached in for a tiny piece of ancient fabric preserved in an air-tight plastic container. Dr. Abrams clipped the soiled, cloth fragment beneath the microscope.

He studied it through the lens and found a single microscopic cell. He methodically scraped it from the material and placed it into regeneration gel inside a petri dish. He affixed the label, "JC" and slid over the next box.

Dr. Abrams peeled off the label "Washington, D.C." and opened the box. He pulled out a woolen collar of an antiquated, fleece shirt, saturated in blood. He extracted tiny blood cells from between gunpowder marks, wiped them into another chemically-soaked petri dish and wrote on the label, "AL".

Dr. Abrams dragged out the final box labeled "Munich, Germany". He tore off the adhesive tape and using sterilized tongs, snagged a glass-encased slide of powdered skull shards. He examined the contents under an electron microscope and found a speck housing a dried skin cell. Dr. Abrams collected the fragment, dipped it into gel and signed, "AH".

He gathered up the specimens and initiated the process of duplication, regeneration and growth then spliced them into zygotes.

Inside the hospital, Detective Nash strengthened his arms and legs. His body learned to accept the hardware and mesh skin grafts without rejection. He figured half of him was synthetic.

Weeks later, medical practitioners deemed fit his release. A male nurse helped him into the wheelchair and they left the room.

"I spotted you this time, Jason."

"Only because I'm wearing the same outfit."

"You mean you've been back?"

"Twice as a janitor and once as a doctor."

"You're good. Why are you contacting me?"

He whispered in his ear as he rolled him toward the elevator, "I know the real story."

Detective Nash looked over his shoulder and asked, "What real story?"

Jason pushed him into the elevator and spoke as the doors closed, "The nuclear story that you and I survived."

"How did you live?"

Jason waited for the elevator to stop, rolled him out and wheeled him down another corridor, "I sat beside your friend in the patrol car. I left after the blast knocked us down the street and ejected me into the woods."

"What do you remember of that day?"

"You and your partner arrested me and a homeless man for being in the wrong place at the wrong time."

"Wrong place, indeed, next to a fresh corpse."

"They solved that case. Dov's going to jail. Like I said, wrong place, wrong time."

"Go on."

"Me and my fellow agent, the guy dressed as a bum, dragged that reporter to the front of the capital building."

"So I did catch you in the act. Why are you telling me this? I could arrest you right now."

"Because I dragged her there after she was killed in the White House."

Detective Nash stopped the wheelchair with his feet, "I thought Dov killed her."

"The White House set him up to take the fall."

"Do you realize what you're admitting to?"

"They tried to kill me that day. They sent me there to dump that body knowing full well that I should have been killed in the blast. They are trying to kill me now."

"Who?"

"The CIA's assassination ring, the Silent Shotguns."

"That's nothing but a legend."

"They're real alright. You know why they use shotguns?" Jason answered his own question, "They use shotguns because even a miss is a hit. Shotgun blasts leave nothing for a doctor to sew together. All the blood cannot be stuffed back in."

"You believe those spook stories?"

"They're silent because you never hear them coming. They're already there. One guy they killed, I heard one of the Silent Shotguns sheet-rocked himself into a wall with a scuba mask, MREs and re-breather tank. He waited a week sealed in a wall to kill his target. They bury themselves in the ground, live in trees, hide in ceilings. Modern-day ninja assassins."

"They're trying to kill you to sever the link between that girl, you and the White House?"

"No, pay attention, they pinned that on Senator Dov Israel."

"Then why are you in danger?"

He pushed the detective into a dimly lit, empty hospital room, "9/11."

"I knew I remembered you. You and I crossed paths that day. Again, you were in the wrong place and definitely the wrong time."

He pulled up the parking brake and stood in front of Detective Nash, "So you do remember arresting me on 9/11?"

"Back during my Jersey days, I busted in your head. You're lucky, your political friends bailed you out."

Jason pushed down the brake, grabbed both grips and pushed him toward the exit, "You can solve it."

"9/11?"

"I'm not saying anything else."

"You want protection then?"

"Protection by who? You, no thanks. Look where you are, you cannot even protect yourself."

"What do you want then?"

"Information on Dr. Abram's experiments."

"Experiments?"

Jason crouched down before the detective, "His cloning experiments."

"What cloning experiments?"

Jason looked back and forth, "He obtained a fragment of Adolf Hitler's skull."

"He's cloning the Fuhrer? That's what you're saying? Tell your boss to stop relying on the National Enquirer for Intel."

"This is a personal mission. Bring me information on Dr. Abram's experiments. In return, I'll give you 9/11."

"Give me what about 9/11?"

"Everything."

He nodded, "I'll check out the doctor first. If I find anything, we'll be in touch."

"If you need me, room 412 at the Hyatt."

Detective Nash wrote it down. Jason pointed at the note.

"Not 214... 412."

"Just sit tight and I'll see you there."

Jason left him in a wheelchair outside the emergency entrance of the hospital, removed his nurse scrubs, threw them into a duffel bag and disappeared into an underground garage.

BlackJack pulled up moments later in the patrol car with sirens and lights blasting. He guided the wheelchair toward the backdoor and lifted him by his armpits into the patrol car, "Who's your friend back there?"

"Just a nurse. Shut those damn sirens before my head explodes."

BlackJack flipped off the switch and seat-belted him in, "I'll take you home and you can get some rest."

"Bring me to the office."

"No way, you're on bed rest for the next few weeks. Doctor's orders."

Detective Nash shook his head, "Bring me downtown."

"Not that nonsense about the girl again."

Detective Nash pulled a Marlboro from his breast pocket and dangled it in his mouth, "You're right for once, forget the office. I need to visit a doctor."

"No problem. I know a great rehab specialist, works on everyone at the precinct."

"It's not for me."

"Then for who?"

Detective Nash lit up the cigarette, "For another case I'm working. Drive me to the research hospital on Main and let me out."

"Can't do it. You need rest."

"Then drop me off at home and I'll drive myself."

BlackJack grabbed the cigarette out of his mouth and snapped it in half., "You're just out of surgery, take it easy."

"Because you quit smoking, now I have to."

"I also quit cursing."

"Right." He lit up another smoke.

"You're an f'n mess. I'm taking you home."

BlackJack ripped the cigarette from his mouth and threw it out the window, "Stubborn bastard, that's why you have no friends."

"I never had friends, only future enemies."

CHAPTER IV

Nine Months Later...

A young, tender, pregnant woman, screened for disease, family history and Caucasian bloodline, rested in a wheelchair with a sedative IV drip. Nurses prepped the equipment, sterilized it and parted as the physicians entered.

The head surgeon examined long films of sonograms and spoke to the medical team while pointing at glossy photos with a pencil, "Triplets, let's see, we have Baby JC, here in front, Baby AL, next in line to the back left and hiding behind to the right, Baby AH."

He flipped through the charts, "Everything looks good. Mother's name, Mary. Exactly forty weeks. Any prior c-sections?"

A nurse answered, "None."

"Bring her in."

Pair of nurses wheeled in the young lady with her protruding, moving stomach. The immature woman dazed in and out of consciousness as tiny legs kicked her innards. Small arms pushed up, forming hands on her stretched skin, tiny, little fingers reaching for life.

A nurse leaned into her ear, "Mary, honey, is there a father waiting outside?"

She nodded and fazed out again.

The lead doctor motioned toward the swinging doors.

"Check pre-op for the father."

Nurses hustled away and returned moments later.

"Nobody there."

Another physician cracked, "Must have been an immaculate conception."

Nurses over-did their shared laughter in the same way they pretended to enjoy the Phil Collins music during surgery, as if the doctors were just regular guys in a bar and not arrogant pricks with a God complex.

An anesthesiologist grabbed the patient's forearm, lifted it and let it drop to the bed.

"She's out. Let's deliver some babies."

They strapped each bare foot into a stirrup, pried her legs apart and marked several incision points, forming a cross. The physician assistant turned up both knobs on the late 80s stereo as nurses and doctors began their dance. Handing him this, handing her that, passing him this, passing her that, all in rhythm with Phil Collins' "I don't care anymore". They careful sliced beneath the bulging belly, removed excess blood and tissue as a purple infant flowed out, greeting the room quietly with both arms up.

"Baby JC, slid right out."

Nurses clutched him, clipped him, cleaned him, clothed him and cleared him away to the closest warming table.

The nurse weighed the pint-sized infant, "3 lbs, 3 ounces."

One of the team doctors peeked over the hanging divider sheet, "Bring him to NICU, stat."

Medical staff rushed the silent infant into an incubator.

"Poor little guy practically fell to the ground as I was cutting. He couldn't wait to enter the world."

They moved him from flesh walls to plastic ones.

"Needs a little weight, that's all."

The doctor smiled and disappeared behind the partition, "Back to work."

He fished around inside her belly and hooked the next baby.

"Another arriving."

He yanked out the shriveled prune.

"Baby AL, got him. He's out."

Nurses wrested the wailing newborn, washed him, wiped him, wrapped him and weighed him while carefully walking him to another waiting warming table.

"Weight, 5 lbs, 6 ounces."

"Heavy for a triplet."

Doctors forcefully pushed around the stomach, causing unconscious groaning from the young lady.

"I see the last one. He's behind something."

An assisting physician jumped in, "Umbilical cord, umbilical cord. It's wrapped around his throat."

"Heart rate's falling. Pull him out."

They sedated the mother further and crosscut her open deeper. The serpentine umbilical cord snaked around Baby AH's neck, squeezing tighter and tighter.

Nurses monitored the heart rate, "Still falling."

"Untangle it, cut it, pull him out."

"Heart rate dropping faster."

They fought the coiled cord and carefully pried open its stranglehold. Doctors grabbed the infant's curled, purple leg and freed him.

"Snagged him. He's alive."

The little raisin screamed and screamed, drowning out su-su-Sussudio.

"Another, 5 lbs, 6 ounces."

Nurses bathed the babbling baby, bundled him, and baked him under a warming table beside his older brother.

Monitors in the room blared and red lights flashed.

"Not done yet, mother's heart rate decreasing quickly."

Doctors tapped her on the hands.

"Stay with me, Mary."

He checked the bank of computer screens.

"Wake up, Mary, Mary."

The lead doctor lifted her chin upwards and tilted her head back, listening and feeling for a breath.

"Wake up girl."

Another doctor placed the heel of his hand on the middle of her breastbone and covered it with the other. He compressed her chest as the other physician pinched both nostrils and exhaled into her lungs.

"More pressure."

"Come on Mary, come back to me."

"We're losing her."

"Keep up the pressure."

They injected her with prescription drug cocktails.

"More, more."

Another doctor slapped her face, "Snap out of it, Mary, snap out of it."

"Grab the defibrillator."

Doctors grabbed charged paddles from the wall and shocked her. Her lifeless body jumped from the gurney.

"Again."

They pushed the paddle on to her chest.

"Hit her again."

Her pulse rate raced to zero and lines on the heart beat monitor straightened out.

He physically shook her.

"Come on, Mary, come back to me. Your sons...what will they do without you? Come back to me."

Flat-lines ran parallel across the computer banks and monotonous tones dominated the silent operating room. Long after clinical death, doctors took turns frantically pushing on her chest, shocking her heart and exhaling into her mouth. Ruler straight lines ran to infinity.

Baby Adolf Hitler, minutes old, claimed his birth mother.

Hours later, Dr. Abrams stared at his creations through the nursery glass. Baby Hitler's jet black hair stood out against his pasty white skin. Toddler Lincoln's wrinkled forehead frowned into hairy cheeks and his pale skin blended into the white-and-blue-striped hospital receiving blanket. Infant Jesus glowed with a bronzed middle-eastern hue. His hair stood on edge, longer and darker than his brothers.

'*He doesn't look like a deity to me*,' thought Dr. Abrams.

St. Christopher's Hospital released Toddler Lincoln and Baby Hitler within a week. Infant Jesus remained in intensive care.

In the police station downtown, BlackJack threw stacks of papers on the desk.

"Check out these newspapers and magazines."

He fanned the batch of periodicals.

"Every single one, without fail, blame the bombing on Pakistan."

Detective Nash picked up a copy of Popular Mechanics and scanned the magazine.

BlackJack continued, "You said you wanted evidence, here it is...in bunches."

He lifted up each magazine and announced it, "TIME, Newsweek, Popular Mechanics, Congressional Quarterly..."

He grabbed newspapers, "Wall Street Journal, New York Times, Washington Post. They all blame Pakistan for the nuke. Let your conspiracies go."

Detective Nash dumped them into the garbage, "You still read newspapers?"

"I came prepared for that."

BlackJack sat his laptop on the desk.

"Here's some online material, all blaming Pakistan for nuking us. Say what you want about the newspapers, at least they are sourced"

He opened a page, "I hardly call quotes from 'anonymous officials' as sources."

"Are you one of those people?"

Detective Nash tossed aside the remaining periodicals, "Those people?"

BlackJack twirled his finger by his ear, "Conspiracy loons. JFK, fake moon landings...all that nonsense."

"What if I could prove it?"

"Fake moon landings?"

"No, what if I could prove another conspiracy?"

BlackJack raised his arms, "Not that one."

"Yes, that one."

"What now? Hasn't that group been enough of a joke?"

"What if they're right?"

"Do you realize how absurd this all sounds? That movement cannot agree if an airliner hit the Pentagon. They cannot even agree that planes hit the towers. Don't even ask those idiots about the plane in Pennsylvania. Half of them think it landed, the other half swears it's shot down and the last half imagine it never existed."

"That's three halves."

BlackJack smiled, "See, even their math doesn't add up. Those conspirators dishonor the victims of 9/11. Forget conspiracy theories, never forget 9/11."

"Never forget? Whenever I wake up in the morning, the first time I look at the clock, it's 9:11. When I am settling in for the evening, sneak a peek at the time, 9:11. Every call that comes in from dispatch, 911. Every September, 9/11. Every year an anniversary, 9/11, 9/11, 9/11. Forget about forgetting, I wish I could forget."

"Settle down, you're only remembering the times you see that number, not all of the millions of times that you don't. Sounds like a mental hang-up more than a conspiracy. That's all in the past. The world moved on."

Detective Nash slumped into a chair, "I never moved on. 9/11 haunts me. Those guys we bagged on that day were involved."

"FBI cleared them."

"Cleared them, right. Government's up to their eyes in 9/11."

BlackJack stood in front of him, "Where's the proof? Where's the whistle-blower? Don't you understand that the government could never keep 9/11 a secret. Those big-mouths open their yap about everything."

"Same government that managed to keep the A-bomb secret from Vice-President Truman."

"Always an answer with you. All talking, no listening. No use reasoning with you. You know everything."

"Keeping an open mind, that's all."

"Close it, before you're labeled a conspiracy nut. Big government is not out to get you, especially you. They pay your salary, they pay mine. Our government treats us well. Full benefits, excellent pay, lofty retirement. Find a private company's benefits that compare to ours."

Detective Nash sprung up from the chair, "It's not about money and security with me. I need the truth. I demand it."

"Don't bite the hand that feeds you."

He turned toward BlackJack, "I'm searching for truth."

"I'm just looking out for you. I'll help. Talk to me."

Detective Nash motioned him over and spoke in a low voice, "I am about to get my hands on 9/11 documents, real serious shit."

"From who?"

"Can't say."

"Tell me, just in case you end up missing."

"Trust me, I'm safe."

"What should I do then?"

"Sit tight. Stay by your phone and I'll call you soon."

Detective Nash left the police precinct.

Inside the White House, beneath a beautiful high cloud, chem-trail, 'tic-tac-toe' grid pattern, breathing filtered indoor air...

General Barker hovered over the desk, "We cannot let this stand any longer. Time to decide."

President Fremont paced back and forth, wearing thin the rug from his chair to the garden view, "Nuking Pakistan only escalates this situation."

"Once we pointed our finger at them, no choice remains."

"They know."

"Know what?"

"They know what really happened that day." He looked at the ceiling and continued, "ISI knows from their moles in Mossad. We nuke a Pakistan city and retaliatory strikes fall on Tel Aviv within hours."

General Barker spread a map of Pakistan across the President's desk and said, "First, you're assuming we fail to shoot down the missile."

"We both know the Patriot success rate."

"They don't. Anyway, they won't even launch if we jam pack our nuclear submarines into the port of Karachi."

"What if they still press the button?"

"Then our subs transform the entire country of Pakistan into glass."

President Fremont stretched out his arm and touched Israel with a sharpened pointer, "What if Pakistan retaliates, nukes Israel and..."

He lifted the pointer, "...and....and... we just silently reverse out of Karachi port without firing a shot."

"I think I hear what you are saying and you should be careful. They're employed at every level of government, they reside in your cabinet and they protect your ass."

"Protect me?"

"Protect us."

The President beckoned over General Barker by curling his forefinger, "They aimed that missile at me. Every Congressman, Senator and Supreme Court Justice left for Christmas vacation. I remained alone in Washington, D.C. and they knew it."

"We spoke off-the-record with them. If we failed to intercept they intended on disarming the trigger before impact."

"You and I know they threatened me before for trying to close that goddamn Federal Reserve."

General Barker waved his hand, "Time to leave the past behind. You're looking backwards. Focus on the present, focus on Pakistan. Consider your only option."

President Fremont gestured at Iraq, "Always more than one option. How about an invasion from Bagram? Send over troops, kill the leaders, declare victory and leave."

"Kill, rape and such, maybe provoke a response from them. Not the best choice, not the worst. Americans demand an 'eye-for-an-eye', 'nuke-for-a-nuke'."

"Follow me here. We use electro-magnetic pulse weapons from HAARP, knocking out their launchers. Send in fleets of stealth bombers and wipe out anything left standing. Protect Israel with anti-missile defenses then start a ground invasion."

"Too many logistics." He stepped closer to the Commander-in-Chief, "End the conflict in a single day. Nice, clean, tidy. No real mess to clean up. It doesn't drag on."

"World has no stomach for more nuclear volleys."

"World or you?"

"Me, if that's what you need to hear. They targeted me with a nuke. We used nuclear weapons decades ago and eventually they were used on us. No more nukes. Invade through Iraq, I'll take the domestic political heat."

"The world's eyes are watching. Showing weakness never succeeds."

"Then we show mercy."

"Mercy succeeds even less."

President Fremont hesitated then said, "Fine, have it your way. I don't need the headache. Draw up target sites with population numbers, religious locations, radical mosques and potential troublemakers. I'll sign off on it.

If we create a nuclear crisis, let's use the opportunity to rid ourselves of all resistors, foreign and domestic."

"This is God's will."

"His or Israel's."

General Barker ordered the entire armed forces to threat level Delta for the remainder of the year. He picked up the phone, alerted every military branch to stand-by readiness and contacted the CIA.

"It is going down this summer. Settle all scores, foreign and domestic."

"Rex 84?"

"Affirmed, include all levels. Agitators, video producers, writers, bloggers, dissidents, protesters, whistle-blowers, witnesses, architects, engineers, everyone on the Red list."

"Do you further authorize Blue list action?"

"Hold off. Step up their surveillance for subversive activity."

"And the White list?"

"Start their windfall. Increase pay scales, forgive debts, mail out tax rebate checks. Keep them happy, they're with us."

CHAPTER V

Months later...

A family of three entered the airport terminal, walked through metal detectors, were sprayed by radiation scanners, groped by TSA hand-held devices, submitted to facial recognition computers, sensed by body heat sensors, peered into eye composite comparisons, observed by emotion trigger detectors and swabbed for explosive residue.

The father moved through the naked body scanner the fastest. His wife, still curvy in her late forties, took a little longer. Their young daughter hesitated before entering.

The TSA agent peeked around from behind the screen.

"Go ahead dear. Don't be shy."

The 20-year veteran TSA agent stuck his head behind cloth divider and turned on the cameras in his peep show. He pressed his face against the screen as the little girl walked in. He focused numerous cameras on her chest, legs and pelvis. He zoomed in with multiple up-shot lenses as the girl started walking out of the frame. He quickly pressed the 'test' button on the computer screen, an alarm buzzed and a red light lit up.

"Sorry, dear, please go through again. You must be wearing something metal."

The girl handed a Hello Kitty bracelet to her parents and entered the machine again. The TSA agent re-focused the equipment, quicker this time, and grabbed the cell phone camera from his pocket. He snapped off reels of close-up pictures from each angle as he placed his hand into his other pocket.

"You're done, dear. Thank you. Enjoy your flight."

He wasted the rest of his day staring at photos of the girl with polka-dot bows covering her hair and polka-dot underwear covering her, until a younger one came along.

The TSA area commander's voice alerted employees through their earphones in both English and Spanish, "White male on terrorist list, approaching Gate number four. Blanco Gringo, puerta cuatro. Detain with caution."

An overweight, GED equivalent, secondary-English-language-speaking, TSA employee and his white, useless-in-the-private-sector, supervisor tapped the father on his back.

"You and your family have been randomly selected for advanced screening. Kindly follow the TSA officer."

The father looked to his little girl while he whispered to his wife, "Great, these leviathans finally move and they harass us."

He turned his attention to the uniformed guards, "Can I help you gentlemen?"

Another TSA officer rushed up to his face, "Do not cause a scene. Our computer randomly selected you and your family for further screening."

He put up his hands, "Nobody's causing a scene. I'll go. Please spare my family the indignity."

The TSA agent opened his arms, "Whole family, no exceptions. Random sweep."

"Random, right. This has nothing to do with my work, does it?"

The TSA agent shook his head, "I am unaware of your films."

"Films, who said anything about films? Sounds like you're plenty aware of who I am."

"Do not flatter yourself. Our computer randomly selects passengers for additional processing."

"Somehow that TSA computer always," he paused and continued, "randomly," he paused and finished, "selects me and my family for additional screening."

Multiple pairs of mixed gender, mixed minority, TSA officers surrounded the family. A skinny, wiry, fair-skinned, Vicodin-addicted, crystal meth smoking, inter-racial loving, female TSA officer tweaked out and took charge, "Sir, please follow these agents to your line. Your wife and daughter must follow me to their line."

He tightly gripped the hands of his wife and child, "You're not taking my family out of my sight."

Her trembling hand reached for the women. "Do not be alarmed. This is standard practice. Federal Law dictates that your wife and daughter need to be screened by female TSA officers."

"You're not separating me from my family."

A brawny, stumpy, muscular, beefed-up TSA agent, who walked with his arms out like a duck carrying luggage, patted his insignia and said, "This means you listen to the lady. Cooperate or we subdue you."

"I'm not going anywhere."

His submissive wife broke her wifely protocol and jumped in, "Just follow him, honey. We've been through this a dozen times. We'll meet at the boarding gate."

Her husband threw down his carry-on bag, "Not this time. I've had enough. They're not taking anyone."

The broad shouldered, thick-necked, barrel-chested, TSA agent crushed a balled fist into the palm of his other hand. The father slicked back his hair, clenched his hands and braced himself.

"Do what you have to do to me but leave my family alone."

His daughter cried and yelled, "Daddy, please stop."

"Princess, nobody is going anywhere."

TSA agents directed the mother and daughter, "Women to the left, men to the right."

His wife urged their daughter to follow her to the screening line.

"Princess, get back here."

His wife pulled the daughter along, "Don't cause a scene. Just follow their instructions and we'll meet you at the Gate."

She guided their daughter toward the line. The father ran for his family, "Come back here."

A meaty, cropped-cut, 8-days-a-week-in-the-gym, TSA agent blind-sided him and forcibly tackled him to the ground. They dragged him from the line. His wife and daughter quivered quietly as they dutifully remained on their screening line.

Onlookers gasped at the commotion, shaking their empty heads as they obediently dropped water, toothpaste, nail clippers, gel shoe inserts, snow globes and scissors into TSA bins and sheepishly waited for their nude internet scan.

His screams reverberated throughout the terminal, "You're not taking my family."

He jerked away from the TSA goon and ran to where his wife and daughter stood. He grabbed each of them by their hands.

"We're canceling our flight. Let's go. We're leaving the airport."

He snatched them from the line. The scrawny, twitching female, assisted by the bulky, 'roid-raged TSA officer, extricated the wife and daughter from his grip.

"Too late, sir. We tried this the nice way but you refused to comply. Your behavior rises to the level of probable cause."

"We're leaving. We're leaving."

The scraggly, TSA agent un-holstered her TASER torture device, "Now, you may not leave."

The burly, husky, beefy TSA agent stepped between them and grabbed the father by his arm. He broke free, scooped up his daughter and bolted for the exit. The TSA agent fired her TASER weapon.

A pair of metal electrodes zipped through the sky leaving wire trials in their wake. They pierced through his clothing and created a current by digging into his skin, shocking him to the ground, dropping his daughter face first onto the linoleum floor, opening a gash above her eyebrow. He flailed helplessly as TSA agents and waiting passengers catcalled and laughed heartedly.

"Turn up the juice."

"Fry, baby, fry."

"See what you get for causing trouble."

"Tase the family next."

Security personnel hurried his wife and child into a secondary screening room. TSA agents, backed up by military units, surrounded him as he bounced around like a fish out of water and hauled him into a dark, square-shaped room, deep below the airport.

Moments later, he regained consciousness, handcuffed to an eyehook protruding from a cement wall. A pair of military men in fatigues sat on chairs, facing him.

"Enjoy producing movies about the government."

He tugged on the handcuffs, "Where's my wife and daughter?"

"Your movies turn citizens against us. Millions of restless subjects, making our job harder. Espousing their so-called rights."

He yanked on the handcuffs again, "I know my so-called rights, bring me to my wife and children."

The military man paced in front of him, "Few questions first."

The father shook his head, "No questions, release me."

"Why do you feel the need to disrupt our job to secure this country?"

"I demand a telephone."

The military man gestured to the other sitting, "Me and my friend here put our lives on the line. Every day. To secure you and your family."

"I don't care. I am invoking my 5th Amendment right to remain silent." He yanked on the cuffs harder, "Go fetch your supervisor, bring him in here."

"My supervisor is the President. I don't think he's available."

The man in fatigues opened a duffel bag and dumped Blu-ray movie discs into a pile on the table. He picked up a few.

"What if you produced documentaries for us?"

"Get my attorney on the phone."

The military man picked up a handful of movies, sorted through them and held up various titles, "Eyes Wide Shut", "Shining", "Clockwork Orange".

"These movies are classics. We feel you could produce classics."

The father smirked, "I'm flattered but no thanks."

"Forget production altogether, direct films. We'll cement your star on Mann's Chinese theater, right next to Stanley Kubrick."

"Again, flattered but no thanks."

"We pay lucratively, offer A-list stars and blockbuster budgets."

"I rather die poor than compromised. No more offers. I'll use my one free call now."

The army man scooped up the discs, placed them in the duffel bag and zipped it up while grabbing another by his foot. He spilled stacks of rubber-banded hundreds across the table.

"IRS, they've been making your life difficult. Take this and go away. Buy a one-way ticket to somewhere in Europe. Try France. That's where everyone goes."

"I am not for sale."

"Everyone's for sale, what's the price?"

"Your heads."

"Wrong answer, especially wrong for someone in cuffs."

He took the cash off the table and tossed it back into the bag. He brandished a pistol from his waistband and laid it down on the tabletop.

"We'll do this the hard way then."

"Whoa, enough mind games, guys. I've been through the good cop, bad cop act. Put the gun away. I am exercising my right to a lawyer."

"Rights. Rights. Do you think we do not know about your rights? We do. We protect your rights."

"Protect them, how, by dragging me and my family in here? By threatening me?"

"We stopped millions of terrorist attacks because we detained a few suspicious people and listened in on a few phone calls. That's a small price to pay for security."

"People who give up liberty for security, deserve neither."

"Then that's what you'll get, neither."

The military man grabbed the weapon and struck him in his temple with the handle while the other crept behind and smothered him with a drawstring plastic bag. The father gulped air as he fogged up the plastic bag. He breathed harder and harder, sucking the bag to his face until it fit like a plastic mask.

"Chop him up, bag the rest of him and stuff him in unclaimed luggage due for incineration."

TSA agents delivered the mother and daughter to a military base area situated inside the airport.

"We'll take over from here."

Military officers grabbed the daughter and separated her from her mother. They carted the mother into an area with a clear tarp floor and discarded of her quickly. If only she wore make-up that day and hit the gym occasionally to return to her pre-child bearing figure. When she lived, her husband used those same complaints as an excuse to carry on affairs.

They gagged and dragged the daughter into a brightly lit, one bedroom studio apartment set up like a stage. Candles burned on the kitchen table and champagne cooled in ice in a plastic bucket.

"We have a fresh one for you, sir."

They tossed the girl on to a fabric sofa. General Barker, dressed in a velour robe, approached her and touched her soft, shaking face.

"Very nice and tender. Clean her head wound and bring her back in fifteen minutes."

He popped a little blue pill, turned to his men and whispered in their ear, "Dispose of the last one. She was an ungrateful bitch."

"Do you approve?"

"I like this new one just fine."

He sat next to her on the couch.

In the adjacent room, US army trained killers dismembered the little girl's parents into bag-able parts and squeezed them inside unclaimed, leather Samsonite luggage, stacked side-by-side. An empty suitcase, propped next to theirs, waited.

Inside the laboratory...

Pour formula, warm bottle, test on skin, feed, bend over shoulder, pat on back, listen for burp, feed, pat on back, hear burp, clean spit-up, hold upright, un-snap dirty clothes, remove diaper, wipe, untangle diaper from the next diaper, affix diaper, snap, snap, snap, snap buttons on new onsies, repeat three times.

Dr. Abrams barely kept his eyes open as he duplicated the tasks every few hours. Sleep dominated his thoughts like an unattainable attractive mistress. The laboratory door slamming waked him from his daydream, he locked the hidden nursery and squeezed out from behind the bookcase.

"Doc?"

Detective Nash peered around the corner.

"Doc?"

Dr. Abrams lumbered from his office, wearing formula stained clothes, unkempt hair and luggage under each eye.

"Can I help you?"

He flashed his badge, "Detective Nash, investigations unit."

Dr. Abrams grabbed it from him, passed it by his face and returned it, "Am I in some sort of trouble?"

Detective Nash traversed the lab, "No. Just a few questions."

"What about?"

He removed a Chemistry textbook from the wall bookcase and thumbed through it, "Nothing in particular. You do research here?"

"This is a lab."

He returned the book to its resting home, "I noticed. What kind of research do you do here?"

"Culture research, microbiological work, cell examination, epidemiologist work, standard lab work."

Detective Nash scanned the equipment and asked, "Is this facility outfitted to clone human beings?"

He rubbed his eyes, "Why do you ask?"

"Just answer the question."

While yawning, "No, we cannot clone in this facility."

"Why not, with all this equipment?"

"No incubator, no state license, no funding."

Detective Nash strolled around the office, touching every item, "Reliable sources inform me that you're cloning human beings."

Dr. Abrams snapped awake, positioned himself between his equipment and the detective, "They don't sound reliable to me. I suppose you will produce a warrant for the search I am watching you conduct."

Detective Nash sifted through papers on a table, "Received boxes from Italy, Germany, and the Smithsonian, did you?"

Dr. Abrams gathered up the papers and locked them in a drawer, "Going through my mail, searching my office without a warrant, will there be any of my Constitutional rights you won't be violating today?'

"We'll see, if you keep it up."

"Is this an interrogation? I didn't hear Miranda."

"Miranda? I am not placing you under arrest."

"This is a private facility funded with my own money."

"You mean your parent's money, right?"

"I was unaware that inheritances are a crime."

"They are if they're used for criminal activities."

Dr. Abrams stepped in front of the detective, blocking him from the desk, "This illegal search is a criminal activity. Our government is a criminal activity. Before I became a physician, I counseled veterans returning home from the Afghanistan War. These vets resented the treatment they received when they came home. The government denied them healthcare, denied them homes, denied them benefits, denied them dignity. The government treated them as if it were better for them to die in that desert nightmare."

"I'm a vet, that didn't happen to me."

"I counseled the ones it did happen to. They turned their rage on their employers, their fellow workers, their wives and their kids. I changed that."

"So you cured them of their violence?"

"No, I pointed them in the right direction. His wife and kids were never the problem. The government, that's their problem. I told them that if they wasted their life then waste it becoming a martyr. Don't orphan your children, orphan your government."

"Am I to interpret that as a threat?"

"Interpret it any way you want."

"You'll have to do better than that."

Dr Abrams walked to the entranceway and tapped on a sign, "Read the door, private property. I do not consent to this search."

Detective Nash half-smiled, "I know this is private property. I sympathize with you. I don't even like asking this but it will help me in solving another case. A case that would change history."

"So you intend to violate my rights to protect someone else's rights?"

"Please, I beg you, cooperate. Someday, you'll look back at this moment and realize that you did the right thing. I'll ask one more time, are you cloning people here?"

"My answer, for the third time, is still no." He held open the door, "Time for you to leave."

Detective Nash said while walking out, "I'll be back with those warrants."

Dr. Abrams followed him down the hall, "Interrogate people with probable cause of a crime. Even if I were cloning, it's legal."

"It's not that you're cloning, it's who you're cloning."

Jason Schwartz ducked down in his car, slightly lifting his head above the window sill. He watched Detective Nash slowly stroll out of the building tailed by Dr. Abrams shaking his fist. Dr. Abrams yelled from the cement stoop about long-gone rights as Detective Nash rode out of the parking lot. Dr. Abrams watched the detective's car disappear down the road and headed back in to feed the boys lunch. Jason caught the door at the last moment and followed him in.

He tapped him on the shoulder.

"Anyone would kill him, you know that."

"Another freaking cop, are you guys kidding?"

"I am no cop."

"You're not with that detective?"

"No."

Dr. Abrams stopped and turned, "You messed up already pig. How did you even know a detective was here?"

"Ok, I concede, I am no pig though. In fact, I hate pigs as much as you."

Dr. Abrams nodded, "No pigs, I get it. You're a Jew, so am I. Shalom and get lost cop."

"We are one, you and I. You know the saying, we must hang together or surely we'll hang separately."

Dr Abrams reached inside his white lab coat for a pistol and clutched it, "Who are you?"

"It is our people against the world. Learn your history, my friend. If you ignore history, you ignore what has happened to your mother, father, sister and brother."

"What do you want with me?"

"Not with you…from you."

"What do you want from me?"

Jason put his arm over the doctor's shoulder in a partial hug, "Any self-respecting Jew would have killed him before World War II."

"Killed who?"

"Don't play dumb. Give him to me."

Dr. Abrams pushed him off his shoulder and pulled the gun from beneath his scrubs, "Not today...friend."

Jason backed up against the wall, opened his jacket and held both arms up, "Don't act hasty. I am unarmed. Let's talk, one Jew to another. Allow me to appeal to your conscience."

"Go ahead," Dr. Abrams lowered the barrel to the ground.

"You know how every Jew asks himself the question of whether he'd kill Hitler if the chance presented itself. If he somehow knew what an adolescent Hitler grew into, would he kill him before he became Hitler?"

"I, too, struggled with such a notion."

He tapped his heart with his hand, "I dwelled on that question every night after stories about my grandmother at Auschwitz. I always assured myself that no sacrifice was too great to rid the world of Hitler, including my life."

"I wish I could help."

Jason approached Dr. Abrams closely and studied his breathing, eye dilation and speech patterns.

"We know he exists. We know you created him."

Dr. Abrams turned away, "He will not be Hitler. He will not see as Hitler saw. He will not speak as Hitler spoke. He will not learn as Hitler learned. He will not feel as Hitler felt. He will not take which Hitler took."

"You could never guarantee that."

"Even if he showed tendencies, we'd manage him. Spend time studying his phrenology, learn about his psyche and analyze him in a controlled manner."

Jason balled both fists, "It's against nature. It's against your people."

"We could turn him. He could save us. His political prowess, economic genius and powerful oration skills directed with the proper guidance will save the Republic. Rescue these United States from tyranny."

"Do you hear how ridiculous you sound? Hitler save us from dictatorship? Might as well have Jesus save Judaism...which we also know about."

"He stays. They all stay."

Jason banged his fist on the wall, "Why any of these abominations? What suicidal Jew creates Jesus?"

"I figured we owed them one, after taking the original."

"You talk so lightly of these serious issues facing your people."

"A sequel to the American revolution is coming. These men will lead it. Jews must be on the right side against this tyrannical government. I know I will."

"You traitor."

Dr. Abrams brandished a Luger pistol from his waistband, "All Jews are not Zionists. Remember your history, Italians took down the mafia, Irishmen stopped the IRA and Japanese crushed the Yakuza. Just like many fellow Jews, I seek to destroy Zionism. It's never about race or religion, it's basic human rights."

"We owe our lives to the land that protects us all."

"I do not argue that. I'm talking about America. You're talking about Israel. I am an American, first. Jew, second."

"Is that how your parents taught you?"

"Leave them out of this."

"They leave you money but fail to teach you about sacred oaths."

Dr. Abrams pointed the gun at his head, "Leave my parents out of this."

Jason turned and walked out of the laboratory while talking. He knew a Jew would never shoot another Jew in the back.

"Stop these experiments before you damn your whole race."

Dr. Abrams escorted him out of the building, "I'm saving my race. It is you and your kind who have damned them."

Dr. Abrams pushed him down the wheelchair ramp outside of the building, "Never come back here. Pass that message along to your detective friend."

Jason picked himself up from the ground, "You pull a weapon on one of your own. You mongrel sell out. Even with your sick experiments, Israel would welcome you with open arms. And what do you do for Israel?"

"Saving America, saves Israel."

CHAPTER VI

Summer...

General Barker and President Fremont stood before the Doomsday device. They each scanned in their palms, completed retina identification and stuck coded keys into computer slots.

General Barker set longitude and latitude coordinates into the computer mainframe.

"You set?"

President Fremont released the key, "I don't know if I can do this."

"Everything's in motion. We cannot turn back now. Newspapers already printed up headlines for tomorrow's edition."

He guided the key out of the lock, "Everybody knows."

General Barker patted him on the back, "We're covered. A few minutes from now, Pakistani terrorists denote explosives in the Mall of America. We launch the missile with full public support."

"They didn't nuke us. Doesn't that count?"

"Everyone thinks they did. Perception is reality."

The President dropped to his knees, closed his eyes and prayed to God. He prayed and prayed and prayed. With each prayer, he closed his eyes tighter and tighter until he forced out tears. His face reddened as he mouthed words with no sound. His jaw clenched as he locked his inflamed hands in prayer firmer.

General Barker waited and waited.

"We need to make a decision. Local news started reporting hearing explosions in the mall."

President relaxed all his muscles, "Bark, I swear I received an answer."

"An answer?"

He opened his eyes slowly, "A voice."

"Whose voice?"

"God's."

"What did he say?"

"He didn't say a word, right away. He led me by the hand and guided me to a futuristic world filled with peace and harmony. No religious battles, no racial hostilities, no class envy, no turf wars, no conflicts at all. I asked him how to get there from here."

"Did he answer?"

"He said, 'Pray and follow your path.', so I will."

President Fremont pulled himself from the crouched position and inserted his key into the computer mainframe.

"Ready, one, two, three."

They both turned their keys simultaneously while computers re-scanned their retinas, fingerprints and facial composition.

The IBM computer's female, sexy, robotic voice spoke, "Identifications confirmed. Location confirmed. Missile launch in ten...nine...eight... seven..."

The Earth shook and tore apart as an empty, broken down barn, in the middle of a corn field, slid sideways across hidden tracks, steel interlaced covers separated, slowly revealing the nuclear missile silo. Sunlight penetrated the opening for the first time in decades. Fresh oxygen filled the hollowed ground. Plumes of fire and smoke glistened off the shiny, metallic exterior and exited through elastic funnel cones on the rear of the projectile. The missile grudgingly awoke from a deep slumber and reluctantly climbed out of the silo into the sky.

Karachi, Pakistan befell the same fate as Palestine and existed only in Arab folklore from here to eternity.

Snap, snap, snap, Dr. Abrams dressed the trio. Gently placed their heads inside the neck-hole of the onesies, snapped shoulder buttons, snapped the buttons on the back, guided their squirmy octopus arms through both sleeves, yanked the garment down to their feet and snapped across the legs and thighs. He immediately reversed the process, changed another diaper and started again.

Feedings occurred hourly. Baby Hitler demanded to be fed before all others. The newborn wrestled his bottle from his father's hands and ingested food fast and furious. He tossed empty bottles across the playpen before Infant Jesus started eating. Baby Hitler vomited constantly from gulping more liquid food than his stomach could handle. His eyes always deceived his stomach. Baby Hitler maintained constant states of colic, even past his younger years.

Toddler Lincoln drank slowly, a few ounces here, a few ounces there while staring vacantly at the 'glow-in-the-dark' sticker stars pasted to the ceiling. Every so often, Baby Hitler smacked him in the back of the head causing the bottle to fly out of his mouth, spilling across the playpen. Baby Hitler deviously gummy-smiled as Toddler Lincoln wailed and wailed while waiting for a refill.

Infant Jesus refused to allow Dr. Abrams to feed him first. He ate enough to grow and saved the remainder of his bottle, offering it to Toddler Lincoln after each encounter with Baby Hitler. Baby Hitler never raised a hand to Infant Jesus during feeding time, no matter how long he sipped the bottle.

The boys slept at random intervals during the early morning, morning, late morning, noontime, afternoon, early evening, evening, late evening, nighttime, midnight and into the next day. Baby Hitler refused to sleep through the night. He worked under cover of darkness, staying up all hours, rolling on his back then to his front, back, front, back, front, bumping into every crib wall while grating his little chubby hands back and forth like a prisoner grinding a metal tea cup across prison cell bars.

As days passed, Baby Hitler spastically army-crawled to-and-fro covering the entire area of his crib, reaching out between the wooden slates toward Lincoln's crib. Toddler Lincoln calmly mimicked the action.

Every Sunday morning, Infant Jesus escaped from his confines, leaving behind his onesie outfit and curled up in the middle of the playroom wearing Croc sandals and a Huggies diaper.

During playtime, both Toddler Lincoln and Baby Hitler ganged up on Infant Jesus, pushing him around, taking his stuff and slapping him in the cheek. Infant Jesus, true to form, turned his cheek, inviting Baby Hitler to slap again. Baby Hitler rarely passed on the opportunity. Still, Infant Jesus offered toys, rattles and his rubber pacifier to his brothers. This only led to more beatings until Dr. Abrams stepped in and separated the trinity.

Lately, Baby Hitler increasingly attacked Dr. Abrams when he split them apart. Dr. Abrams knew he wasn't the most threatening guy but this infant was far too young to rise to Alpha Wolf. He needed to control him better.

Dr. Abrams evaluated the children daily, checking their height, weight, circumference of their head, skin color, hair color, eye color, teeth growth, language skills, diction, motor skills, dexterity and memory. He absorbed volumes and volumes of historic records, text books, under oath testimony, hearsay, versions of the Bible, texts of the Koran, New Testaments, Old

Testaments, autobiographies, semi-auto biographies, unauthorized biographies, articles, columns, editorials, all to understand his sons from the actions of their clone fathers.

Baby Hitler always scored the best, his actions most resembling the way his DNA donor developed. Infant Jesus scored the worst.

Dr. Abrams expected more from his Jesus clone. He spoke last, ate last, rolled over last, crawled last, stood last, ate solid foods last, everything last. Dr. Abrams noted in the daily diary, "*None too sure about JC's success. Other two growing, acting and behaving more as the donor.*"

Dr. Abrams read books and solved shape puzzles with Baby Hitler and Toddler Lincoln while Infant Jesus busied himself tossing plastic, baby clothes coat-hangers into the garbage. Dr. Abrams encouraged the throwing ability and played catch with Infant Jesus. He rolled the ball to Infant Jesus' left hand and coaxed him to throw it back. He figured if this is not the reincarnation of Christ, he might as well teach him to play baseball, preparing him as a left-handed, 7th inning, one-batter, situational reliever, earning a few million annually, while keeping down the wear-and-tear on his arm by pitching sixty innings a year.

Dr. Abrams missed the buzzing noise and flashing iridescent light as he fixed bottles. He heard the lab door open, jumped from his chair and scrambled to close the hidden bookcase. He rushed into the playroom, only to freeze in his tracks when he saw Detective Nash cradling Infant Jesus in his arms.

"No cloning here, right?"

"These are my sister's babies."

Detective Nash lifted the bassinets one-by-one with his free-hand, reading the monograms, "Baby AL, Baby CJ, I mean JC, and Baby AH. That's a coincidence, your sister just happened to name her kids Abe Lincoln, Jesus Christ, and Adolf Hitler."

"What do you want?"

"Lying to an authority is a felony," said Detective Nash as he returned Infant Jesus to his crib.

Dr. Abrams opened his arms wide, squeezed the cribs together and pushed them against the wall, "Nothing to hide here. Everything's legal. You want to know what's not legal, breaking into my lab and harassing me. Yet, here you are again, behaving as if I am the criminal."

"These three clones, they are who I said they are?"

Dr. Abrams nodded, "Meet my sons."

"They are not your sons, they are clones."

Dr. Abrams slipped a torn coloring book page from beneath a magnet stuck to a petri-dish refrigeration system, "Look at this drawing from Baby

Hitler. Admittedly, he colored outside the lines but he's barely able to hold the crayon."

"You're trying to convince me that this is Hitler's clone?"

He returned the sketch to the refrigerator, "I only can convince you of my love for my sons."

"These are not natural sons." He pointed to Infant Jesus, "That is not God's son," pointed to Baby Hitler, "That is not the devil's son," pointed to Toddler Lincoln, "That is not America's son. These are all experiments gone wrong."

"I love them as my children."

"They are as human as an aborted fetus, no natural rights, no legal rights."

"Man's law does not protect them, God's law does."

Detective Nash flashed his badge, "I work in Man's law and our law defines these things as clones. You know that cloning may only be utilized for organ transplant. Hearts, lungs, eyes, kidneys and such."

Dr. Abrams lifted Infant Jesus, "Body harvesting, that you consider natural."

"I don't write the laws, I enforce them. These clones must be used for aiding a diseased person or they must be destroyed."

He lifted the newborn higher, "Destroy Jesus, a catholic authority figure instructs me, a Jew, to kill Jesus. I will not repeat the sin of my forefathers. I will speak up. Jesus lives."

"I'm positive he's not Jesus, not even Jesus, Jr."

"How can you be so certain?"

"Well, has little Jesus here performed any miracles?"

"He shares his toys, his food and his clothing."

"Are you sure you're not reading too much into normal baby behavior? Seeking signs that may not exist."

Dr. Abrams picked up a stuffed Dinosaur and dropped it alongside Infant Jesus in the crib. Infant Jesus cried hysterically until he removed it, "There's your proof."

"That's it?"

"He also struggles on science-related tasks."

"Does he walk on water?"

"He did."

"When?"

"Last week, with me...at the ice rink."

"Very clever, somehow I think you know that is not what I mean. There's no proof any of these clones are real."

"You do not need proof, you need belief."

Detective Nash peered into the crib, "Sharing a bottle and disliking stuffed dinosaurs, doesn't prove he's God's son."

"I told you. He's not God's son, he's my son."

"Nothing but clones."

Dr. Abrams pointed at the corner crib, "See young Lincoln over there. He's studious, even as a baby. He cannot even sit up and yet we can't keep him away from building with Lincoln Logs."

"Lincoln logs, did he oppose slavery yet?"

"He'll save us from slavery. My sons will save this great country from our own tyrannical government. We'll do it from the inside-out."

"Save the country, by cloning Hitler?"

"You are obsessed with the Hitler clone and dictatorship." He latched a squirming Baby Hitler into a battery-operated swing, "Yet, you've been reading my mail, tapping my phone and interrogating me without cause."

"That's police work."

He pressed the button and classical music played while the infant swung in an arch, "Each of those police work encroachments of rights led to Hitler, the real Hitler. Not this child."

"Hitler killed millions, can we at least agree on that?"

"He never killed anyone himself. His jack-booted thugs killed. Thugs, like yourself, detective."

"What makes your Hitler clone any different from the original?"

Dr. Abrams popped a pacifier into Baby Hitler's mouth, "Change only occurs by War or Peace."

"So you prepared leaders for both ways?"

"You could say that."

"Why did you need new versions of both Jesus and Lincoln?"

"Peace needed a back-up."

"Peace? Sounds more like War needed a back-up. Lincoln killed far more Americans than Hitler."

Dr. Abrams picked up Toddler Lincoln and squeezed him into a bouncy seat.

Detective Nash folded his hands, "Frankly, I don't believe any of this."

"Nobody's forcing you to believe."

"Enough with this back and forth. I'll cut you a deal. I stop showing up at your office and you hand me the Hitler clone. The other two stay."

Dr. Abrams stood in front of the mechanized swing, "No deal. Arrest me for legally cloning or be on your way."

"I'm not arresting you. Not right now."

"People are drawing up sides, lists are being made, plans are being checked and re-checked. We're waiting for the spark. Revolution is coming. It's coming. These boys will lead it."

"Revolution, what revolution?"

Dr. Abrams strapped Infant Jesus into a walker, "Patriotic Americans hit their tipping point. They cannot sustain this government and their lackeys anymore."

"Who are you revolting against?"

"Who does anyone ever revolt against? Government and their well-paid, well-fed guards. We're trimming the public sector fat. Much like the trimming performed on Louis XVI...little off the top please."

"I work for the public sector and that sounds like a threat."

"Not a threat, it's economics. The working man cannot sustain the government employee with huge salaries, unending benefits and lavish retirements. Revolution does not need me. Taxes started the last Revolution. Funny how history repeats itself."

"Take it up with your Congressman. They control the tax system. Vote them out."

"We agree there. Vote them out and my sons in. These boys keep us from a violent revolution. They'll peacefully carry out a passive revolution from the inside."

Detective Nash shook his head, "They're not even real."

"If you do not believe in them, then there should be no problem."

Detective Nash walked to the exit door and pointed to the infants, "Use these clones for helping disabled people or destroy them. If they're still here by next month, I will arrest you and dispose of them myself."

The Department of Motor Vehicles opened early for once. Newly installed, post-9/11 mindset, automated systems raised red flags whenever a citizen renewed their license and turned up on a 'terrorist list.' States staffed every DMV with specially trained armed forces, lying in wait, for a terrorist. Similar to the system implemented in the airlines where air marshals boarded every flight. Most of the times, it was uneventful for the modern day police cowboy. They passed time by shoving around the elderly, tasering the young and humiliating minorities.

A rural man, who operated a survivalist website, voted for Ron Paul and listened to Hank Williams, Sr. entered the molasses operation to renew his license after several moving violations. Authorities nabbed him in an illegal 'seatbelt' check roadblock and ticketed him for an expired driver's license. This marked his second offense in a week when the local police set up another unconstitutional checkpoint outside of a local bar. He barely avoided the DWI charge after drinking a single shot of whiskey in an entire night.

After several hours waiting on line, watching DMV employees enjoy repeated coffee breaks, multiple outdoor cigarette breaks, constant bathroom breaks, government-mandated fifteen minute breaks and an hour lunch break, the Rural man's turn arrived.

An over-paid, under-height, over-weight, under-qualified, minion worker asked, "Did y'all fill out form MV-44?"

Rural man handed over his paperwork.

"No, that is form DL-44C. Totally wrong."

He responded, "This is what the person at the window told me I needed."

"Linda told y'all that?"

"Whoever the lady at the window over there is," he said as he gestured toward the entranceway.

"She's wrong and you're wrong."

"What about this?"

He pushed another form across the counter, "I filled out this also."

"No that's MV619R, for a renewal."

"I need a renewal."

She handed him another stack of forms.

"You'll have to go back, fill this out and return it to me."

"Can I just complete it here?"

"No, I am on a break after you. Fill it out and another representative will help you."

"It will take me just a few minutes."

"Take your time. I'm on break. Rushing to complete the forms is probably the reason why you filled them out improperly."

Before he responded, she set the 'Next Window' desk sign on the counter and hurried off to smoke a Parliament. He carefully filled in each spot on the form, wrote out a check to the DMV and walked to the back of the line.

Four hours and four satisfied customers later, he approached the window.

"Did you enjoy your coffee break?"

She removed the 'Next Window' sign from the counter, "State law requires mandated breaks during the business day."

"You know, when I worked construction, we never took breaks."

"Maybe you should have educated yourself and you'd be here."

"Ma'am, in our brief encounter, I already know I am ten times more qualified than you to work anywhere at any job. If there weren't any government jobs, you'd be penniless and homeless."

"When I retire, I receive full benefits and three-quarters pay. I'll hire you to tend to my lawn."

He handed over the paperwork, "Just renew my license."

She put it aside and walked to the back room. Another hour later, she returned.

"Let's get started on this renewal, shall we? Please hand over your expired license."

He thumbed through his rubber band wallet and produced the identification. She entered it into the system. Red colors flashed across the screen.

"Hold on."

She raced to the back and woke up the federal guard.

"Code red, line #12."

The waking guard wiped drool from the corners of his mouth, tucked in his shirt and checked his weapon. He stomped out from the backroom and headed directly toward the rural man.

"Sir, you have to come with me."

"For what?"

The guard jumped into a shooter stance, pointed his weapon at the man and yelled, "Follow me or you'll be sorry."

Instinctively, the rural man reached for his packed weapon. The slow-moving, slow-witted security guard failed to fire a shot as a bullet ripped through his chest. He sprawled out on the floor gurgling.

Pied Piper time arrived for the rural man for everyday atrocities committed against him by those in charge. He shot the teller in her fat forehead because he wasted his entire day on line. He blasted another time burglar for the impromptu checkpoints he endured. He annihilated the security guard while remembering the local government official who forced him to tear down an extension on his property due to a building code violation of being a foot too close to the curb. He kicked and fired at a DMV manager for the IRS freezing his bank account due to their own accounting error. He attacked the supervisor in response to CPS stealing his children based on an anonymous tip. He kept shooting and shooting to address grievances with every part of the government. They never acted on his written grievances, so they suffered his physical ones.

Numerous other cops, in full riot gear, goose-stepped in lines, marched in circles, surrounded the area and waited for the shooting to stop. Once the shooter emptied the clip, using the final bullet on himself, they busted into the DMV office and saved the day for a photo-op.

Detective Nash met Jason Schwartz in a tunnel, beneath a bridge.

"We could have met in a public place. No one in intelligence uses tunnels anymore."

"I'll take that under advisement," said Detective Nash as he handed over a briefcase, "Here you go."

He passed Jason numerous detailed papers of the cloning experiments, pictures of the layout of the laboratory, clandestine rooms, false wall locations, duplicate entrance cards and profiles of the staff.

"Where are the documents you promised me?"

"Which do you want, 9/11 or the nuke?"

"I'll take both."

Jason shook his head, showed Detective Nash a red coded key and said, "This key opens a P.O. box across town. Inside it, details and documents relating to the US government's involvement in the 9/11 operation, Big Wedding."

He held up a blue coded key, "This key opens a safety deposit at Bank of America on Lexington Street. That box contains enough evidence to convict Israel in a Washington minute of the nuclear launch."

He checked his watch and continued, "In an hour, all of these documents will be destroyed. You decide, 9/11 or the nuke."

"If I choose the red key then your government escapes attacking America. If I choose the blue key then my government escapes 9/11."

"Even if you expose the nuclear attack on America, I don't expect any retaliation against Israel. Your government will use their selective amnesia, like the USS Liberty."

"Sounds like you're trying to persuade me to solve 9/11."

"I love my native land."

"What if I arrest you right now?"

"Then you solve nothing."

Jason tossed him the keys, walked out through the tunnel and held the stopwatch button on the side of his wristwatch.

"One hour, starting... now."

Detective Nash raced to his car. He peeled out down the street leaving a rubber trail behind him. He ran a red light while dialing his cell phone.

"BlackJack, it's me."

"What do you want, partner?"

"Drive to 128 Lexington Avenue, there's a bank there. Bank of America. Pass by that café where they give us free donuts."

"What's this about?"

"Just get there. I'll be throwing a blue key out of my car. Go to the café, pick up the key and hurry to 128 Lexington. Grab what's inside the safety deposit box number 7-2-9."

"What's in there?"

"I'll explain later. 128 Lexington, asap."

"On my way."

Detective Nash lifted the driver side wheels off the ground rounding a corner and tossed the blue key out his passenger side window. He arrived at the Post Office Box with minutes to spare and hustled inside the building.

His police instinct immediately recognized a pair of out-of-place men trying too hard to fit in, one with a backward baseball cap and boat shoes, the other in a short-sleeve Hawaiian shirt and sandals. Both men hid beneath dark sunglasses, reading newspapers.

Detective Nash searched for the Post Office Box while keeping an eye on the duo. He found the box, stuck in the key and took out reams of papers, discs and audio tapes. This prompted both causally dressed men to send texts.

Across town, BlackJack drove in the usual police manner, breaking all posted speed limits, weaving in and out of traffic and whipping through red lights until he found the key under a sidewalk bench near the café. He pulled into the parking lot near 128 Lexington Avenue.

He spoke into his cell phone, "Made it just under the hour but there's no bank here."

"It has to be there."

BlackJack looked up and down the city blocks, "Nothing, it's a kosher deli."

"Are you at the right address?"

He read his chicken-scratch note, "I wrote it down as soon as you called, 128 Lexington."

Detective Nash checked his spiral notepad, "Negative on 1-2-8, that's 8-2-1 Lexington ...repeat, 8-2-1 Lexington."

BlackJack turned around, stepped on the gas and sped down the street.

He yelled into the speaker phone, "How did you ever make detective with that problem of yours?"

"It only happens when I rush."

"It may cost us today."

"Call me when you're in the vault."

"Gotcha."

Detective Nash threw down his phone.

Moments later it rang again, "I'm in, the deposit box is empty."

"Does it look disturbed?"

"Some swept dust. Something definitely was in here recently."

"Print it, see what comes up."

"Will do. By the way, you girl-tossed the f'n keys into a pricker bush. Nowhere near the coffee shop. I'm sitting here with bleeding hands."

"File a comp claim."

"And give me the right address next time, you f'n dyslexic retard."

Detective Nash closed the flip cell phone, drove wildly to his home to shake any tails and dumped the contents of numerous manilla envelopes across his desk. He examined the labeled contents, CD copies of black box recordings of A.A. Flight #11 and U.A. Flight #175, Air Traffic controllers tapes, classified recorded interviews of the President and Vice-President, official 'Big Wedding' CIA document and blueprints of the World Trade Center Buildings #1, #2 and #7 with nano-thermite sites marked in red ink.

A small note, tucked inside a black box recording fell out as he placed the materials inside his home safe. He opened the folded paper and read the hastily handwritten words:

Celebrate America's Independence at the beginning of every month, until Christmas.

Along the many highway lanes on the Island of New York.

Kicked over the moneychangers tables,

Call him the Dayton Dry Goods Company's heir.

Even with the treasure trove of 9/11 evidence, this note stood out alone. It connected to none of the 9/11 materials. This note related to something else. 9/11 didn't need this note. The other material solved 9/11.

He read each line, again and again. He scratched out algorithms, capitalized every other letter, used codes, replaced letters, assigned numerical values, nothing deciphered the note. The only part he figured out was the third stanza clearly referred to 'Jesus', kicking over the moneychanger's tables.

Celebrate America's Independence at the beginning of every month, until Christmas.

The first stanza caused him to check holidays from July 4 to Christmas. Independence Day, Ramadan, Labor Day, Patriot Day, Rosh Hashanah, Yom Kippur, Sukkoth, Columbus Day, Veteran's Day, Thanksgiving, Hanukkah,

Christmas, a lot of religious holidays. He scribbled on the notepad, maybe that tied into Jesus in the third stanza.

Along the many highway lanes on the Island of New York.

Staten Island, Manhattan Island, Long Island, Ellis Island, Plum Island, Shelter Island, Fire Island. Any other islands in New York? Needed more work, he noted on his pad.

Call him the Dayton Dry Goods Company's heir

Start this part tomorrow, he wrote boldly. The note dominated his waking and sleeping hours. After many days, he convinced himself, forget this note. This scribbling had nothing to do with 9/11. He tucked it into his back pocket. Never forget solving 9/11. Never forget 9/11.

CHAPTER VII

Winter...

Dr. Abrams traveled with the threesome everywhere, at no time, they left his sight. Wal-mart, K-Mart, BJs, Costco, Wal-Greens, Best Buy, Sam's Club, Lowe's, and every other Chinese manufacturing front. Baby Hitler loved Home Depot, Toddler Lincoln enjoyed Barnes & Noble and Infant Jesus' eyes lit up in the A&P.

The trio sat in a grocery shopping cart designed as a race-car, wheeled around the store by their surrogate father. Baby Hitler drove. Toddler Lincoln rode shotgun.

Baby Hitler smirked as he turned the plastic steering wheel recklessly, imagining plowing into other customers, too young to realize that the wheel failed to control the pushcart. The constant frustration caused him to repeatedly launch himself out the plastic car door, landing squarely in the middle of an aisle, accompanied by uncontrollable screaming fits. Other shoppers pretended not to notice, turned around and walked away, avoiding the spectacle, more than a few stayed, watched and listened.

Toddler Lincoln grabbed the wheel during Baby Hitler's tantrums.

Infant Jesus stood behind his brothers, inside the area littered with groceries. He scooped items from the shelves and dropped them into other patron's shopping carts as they passed by.

Inexplicably, each item he dropped into a stranger's cart ended up changing their life. Cookies, saved a dieting diabetic from a seizure on her way home. Baby aspirins, prevented a stressed-out homemaker's stroke. Bottle of water, cooled an overheated engine from igniting.

Dr. Abrams prepared for a diaper change like he prepped for surgery. He scrubbed himself clean, disinfected the changing table, donned a surgical mask and stretched plastic gloves over his hands. Despite all his precautions, he usually ended up neck-deep in soiled diapers. Literally and figuratively, his life went to shit.

His diaper changing technique modeled that of a NASCAR pit crew. Dr. Abrams parked the babies on the changing table, removed their rubber shoes, changed the diapers, cleaned up skid marks, repaired body damage, watched for spills and worked as quickly as possible to avoid noxious fumes.

Jason Schwartz snuck through the facility while ingesting fast-acting, Capecitabine pills which rapidly inflamed both hands, wiping out his fingerprints. He unlocked the laboratory door using a duplicate card-key and crept through the room until he reached a trio of cradles resting on a changing table.

He noticed each cradle draped in monogrammed soft cloths. Jason moved bassinet to bassinet reading the initials. He stopped when he found the name and reached in. He clumsily knocked into an overhead Moon & Star mobile, causing it to start playing music and rotating, captivating the newborn in his own miniature theater. Jason turned the baby over and pressed the barrel of the silencer into the cradle.

"Never again."

Dr. Abrams scrubbed the baby's hair, washed his bottom, powdered him and neatly affixed a brand new diaper. He swaddled the infant then carried him down the hall and into a changing room. Baby Hitler, who already took his bath, stood in the corner of his crib, holding himself up on the railing, with his hair slicked down from tub water, screaming babble in an invective rivaling his DNA donor's Sportpalastrede speech.

Dr. Abrams lowered Infant Jesus into a crib, "Alright little Jesus, all clean. We'll give you back your cradle as soon as I finish bathing little Lincoln."

Dr. Abrams walked over to the bassinet to grab Toddler Lincoln. Dr. Abrams pulled off the soft cloth. He jumped back and fell to his knees. Toddler Lincoln, laid motionless, face down.

He dropped to a prone position on the floor, shook his fist in the air and yelled through streaming tears, "Who killed my son?!"

He stumbled to his feet, grabbing the sides of the cradle to pull himself up. Dr. Abrams reached in and held the dead newborn. He wept and wept as blood ran down his arms and saturated his shirt. He dialed the police.

"Someone killed my son."

He repeated it and repeated it to the police dispatch.

Dr. Abrams searched through the laboratory, upending tables, tossing paper out from desks, and ripping apart folders until he found the business card.

He screamed into the receiver, “Your assassin missed, detective!”

Detective Nash held the phone away from his ear and checked the Caller ID number, “Is this you Dr. Abrams?”

“He missed.”

“What assassin? Missed what?”

Dr. Abrams alternated between crying and yelling, “He killed the wrong baby.”

“Somebody attacked your clone?”

Dr. Abrams sobbed into the phone, “My son. He killed my son.”

“He, who?”

“Whoever it is you work for.”

“You’re not making sense. I do not work for anybody.”

Dr. Abrams halted all emotion, “If I ever see you again, you’re a dead man.”

He hung up the phone.

Detective Nash rushed to a seedy part of town. He found the ‘rent-a-room-by-the-hour’ hotel address given to him by Jason Schwartz, who never slept in the same place for more than a day. He pounded on the door. Jason opened it while yawning and rubbing his eyes.

“What brings you here?”

Detective Nash recognized the act. Every time some loser beat his wife, he pretended to be sleeping. He grabbed him by his undershirt, wrapped it around his neck and pinned him against the wall.

“You killed that goddamn Hitler clone, didn’t you?”

Jason knocked his arms off, “No, no, never. I wasn’t even there.”

“I know you were there. One of my officers tailed you.”

“I wasn’t there.”

Detective Nash firmly placed his hand over Jason’s heart.

“You’re beating a mile-a-minute.”

“What do you expect when you bust in here and toss me into a wall?”

“You were there. Admit it.”

Jason pushed him off, “I didn’t go to shoot anyone. I wanted to reason with him.”

“At the point of a gun?”

“He kept defending reincarnating Hitler. He’s crazy. Hitler must never be resurrected.”

Detective Nash unhooked his handcuffs from the loop on his pants, "I must bring you in."

Jason backed away, "For killing a clone? Clones have no rights. You told me that yourself. They are presumed mere cells for organ harvesting. Any use other than organ replacement is illegal."

"I'm placing you under arrest. Discharging firearms, killing a clone. This is not right."

"Neither is abortion but I don't see you arresting abortion doctors."

Detective Nash shoved the handcuffs into his jacket pocket, "He thinks I sent you there to kill the Hitler clone."

"So what if I killed that clone? If a Jew knew that Hitler would do what he did then should he kill him? You know my answer."

"You may not have, after all."

"What do you mean?"

"You missed."

"I missed?"

"Baby Hitler was in another crib, you missed."

"Another crib?"

Detective Nash retrieved the handcuffs from his pocket, "I cannot let this go. We'll sort this out at the station. I'm taking you in right now."

Jason held up both hands in a stop position, "Hold up. I'll give you the nuke info on Israel and the murder of that girl. They'll kill me in jail."

"No can do."

Detective Nash held out the handcuffs and walked toward Jason when a club strike knocked him to the ground. Thoughts flowed around his brain…

His…

…life…

…passed by…

…as fast.as…

…the turning…

…of…

…a…

…page…

Bright lights shined on his face, Detective Nash shook his head, leathery straps secured him to the chair. He looked around at riveted walls, figuring he sat inside the cargo area of a truck.

A pair of masked men stood on either side of him.

"Do you know who we are?"

"Shotgun Squad."

"They're an old wife's tale. Nobody encases themselves in cement waiting for their victim. That's a fable from the 80's."

"You're Mossad then."

The masked man approached him closer, "Maybe."

"What do you want with me?"

"We need those documents back. Someone stole them from us and handed them to you."

"I don't have any documents."

The masked man back-handed him across the face, "Stop lying."

"I already gave them to every journalist I know."

"We own every journalist you know, so you didn't do that."

The masked man pulled out an Exacto knife.

"Let's start over. Who gave you the documents?"

"An anonymous tipster."

He held the blade near his throat, "Who was this anonymous tipster? Was he the man in the hotel room?"

"Possibly."

He placed the knife on a table near a power drill, "See, you cooperate and everyone's happy. We do not intend to kill a detective. Bad for business. Tell us about this tipster."

"That's all I know. He contacts me."

"Did he ever tell you that he worked for us?"

"He said you betrayed him."

"We betrayed him, more like the other way around. He's insane you know. We cut him loose years ago after he peddled forged documents blaming governments for 9/11. Did he provide you with these fabricated documents?"

"Yes."

"Where are they now?"

"I sent them to the FBI."

"Another lie. You're burying yourself here. Literally, six feet deep."

"I do not have them."

"Always the hard way with you tough guy cops. We know you remember 9/11. You arrested people posing as our agents in New Jersey."

"I remember."

The masked man picked hairs from the back of his head and cut them with the Exacto blade, "You also lost your wife in those towers."

He turned away. The masked man forced his head forward.

"People told you to stop pursuing those leads from New Jersey and you listened."

"I don't listen anymore."

"We'll see about that."

The masked man slashed him across his cheek with the knife. Detective Nash jolted around in the seat as streams of droplets soaked into his shirt.

"Where are the documents?"

"I sent them to police headquarters."

"I thought you sent them to the FBI?"

"I meant the FBI."

"Strike three. Time to apply real pressure."

The masked man plugged in the tarnished, paint-chipped drill with a giant rusted bit. He pressed the trigger and watched the bit ramp up, then rested it at his feet.

"Where are those documents? Last chance."

He struggled with the bindings, "I sent them to the FBI."

The masked man pressed the trigger as the drill whirled into a blur and lowered it to the detective's foot. The drill bit tore open the top of his canvas boot, cut through the tongue and wedged between his metatarsal, cutting half moons into the surrounding foot bones.

Detective Nash released a muffled scream. He thrashed back and forth as his foot stayed pinned to the ground.

"Think about where those documents may be and I'll remove the drill. Lie again and the next one goes through your testicles."

"Take a few moments to decide." The masked men laughed and left.

He heard them lock a chain across the cargo area.

Detective Nash listened for sounds of breathing outside the door. He waited a few minutes then kicked off his other boot, slid his foot along the slick, stained floor until it reached base of the drill. He pushed in the reverse mechanism with his toe and pushed the trigger. The drill spun out from his foot unleashing geysers of blood like a shook-up, popped champagne bottle. The drill locked and cast about wildly across the floor until he reversed it and guided it to the restraints. It ripped apart the leather and steel mesh, freeing his legs.

He stood up and crashed down on the wooden chair with his entire body weight, splintering it to pieces, freeing his hands. Detective Nash heard someone quickly shuffling keys, unlocking the chains and lifting the door handle. He stopped the drill and pressed himself alongside the door.

The masked man busted in and fired shots through the empty chair. Detective Nash grabbed him by the neck, jammed the drill bit into his ear and pulled the trigger. White tissue and brain matter swirled and spit from the side of his head. He collapsed with the drill still rotating. Detective Nash fumbled his way out of the back of the Urban Moving Systems truck and ran for the nearest road.

His blood trail ended at the highway when a passerby brought him to a local hospital. The same hospital and the same exact room he was in before.

"Nurse, listen carefully to me. I'm a police detective, someone's trying to kill me. Admit me under an assumed name, bandage me and alert the sixth precinct."

Doctors cut off his boot, knocked him out, stitched together tendons, muscles and skin then hooked him on prescription pain medications.

Official records indicated that John Doe arrived at the hospital and treated for a foot injury.

The head nurse buzzed his room, "Your precinct on line one."

Detective Nash picked up the phone, "Is BlackJack there?"

"Not in today."

"I've been calling him all week. Where is he?"

"Home sick with the flu."

He hung up, gathered his belongings and arranged for a ride. He tossed his crutches into the cab, flashed the driver a hundred and told him to step on it. The taxi driver drove as if he was qualifying for the Brickyard.

A midnight, black, tinted-window Mercedes shadowed every turn.

Detective Nash arrived home, threw the cabbie a crisp bill and hopped on crutches into his house, rushing to an enormous basement safe, capable of housing an entire illegal alien family.

He unlocked the drawer, grabbed the combination and spun the dial, *"48...15...no wait."*

He reset the knob to zero, *"15...48...34."*, and pulled the metal bar, it barely budged.

"51...48...34 or is it 43?"

He held the paper an arm length away from his face.

Detective Nash heard a car door slam, he peered out the barred basement window and saw a figure exit the black vehicle parked sideways in his driveway. He grabbed the pistol from his waistband and rested it on the floor next to him.

"Calm down, you've opened this safe a thousand times."

He blocked out all distractions and re-read the numbers.

"48...51...43, here we go."

He heard the downstairs door creep open and started spinning the dial again.

"48...51...34"

Faint clicking noises emitted from the lock as tumblers dropped into place. He kept one hand on the safe and trained the other on the door with handgun in tow.

Detective Nash twisted the door handle and yanked open the heavy metal door. He heard the distinct sound of a shotgun being cocked.

"BlackJack."

"Drop the pistol."

Detective Nash set the gun on the ground and looked into the safe, staring down the double barrel of a dark, 12-gauge shotgun.

"You're CIA, Shotgun Squad."

"Guilty as charged."

"You dirty son-of-a-bitch. You ate dinner at my house. You attended my church. You grieved with me when I lost my wife. You were my partner."

"Nothing personal. I meant those things but I must live up to my oath."

"You sold your soul to Mossad then?"

"No, the Shotgun Squad is their American mirror. We set them up. They're so busy conducting their wars through deception, they failed to consider we'd use it on them."

"I've known you for years."

"They assigned me to you. Anyone in a position of power has one of us minders. You learned too much my friend. You crossed the line."

"Line, what line?"

"We couldn't let you reveal 9/11, not you and your Jewish friend."

He lifted the barrel to eye level, "9/11 opens the can of worms of Oklahoma City, which opens the can of worms of WACO, which opens the can of worms of JFK, which opens the can of worms of USS Liberty, which opens the can of worms of Pearl Harbor, which opens the can of worms of the Federal Reserve, it would never end. The gaping holes those worms created could never be filled in. Our government could not survive those revelations. So it won't."

He pressed the barrel to Detective Nash's forehead, "Goodbye, I always considered you a good cop."

A voice from the darkness screamed, "Duck."

Detective Nash dropped free-fall to his knees.

Guns fired. Smoke clogged the room. As the fumes cleared, BlackJack, with a scuba tank on his back, slumped motionless over the shotgun, propping him up as the barrel lodged into the ground. His rigid fingers cradled the trigger.

"You saved me. I thought you were trying to kill me."

Jason patted him on the back, "Trying to kill you? I signed my own death warrant when I revealed 9/11."

"Then why were you chasing me?"

"I uncovered his identity weeks ago. I trailed you to stop you from opening this safe. He laid in wait for about a week."

"That explains the air tanks, MREs and re-breather."

"Guess the rumors are true about encasing themselves in sheet-rock."

Detective Nash pushed aside BlackJack's body and grabbed the 9/11 evidence.

"Your Mossad friends worked me over."

"They're not my friends and they're after me too."

"I owe you one."

"Then owe me one now and forget about that clone mistake."

"That's asking a lot."

"I saved your life and gave you 9/11 on a silver platter."

"Alright, that crime dies with me. Truly, I understand wanting to kill Hitler before he became Hitler. Promise me, no more attempts on that clone, let the police take care of it."

"Agreed."

"We're even then."

Jason closed his hands in prayer, "Just one more wish, please."

"Go ahead."

"Permit me to be there for the 9/11 arrests."

"Deal."

They shook on it. He held up the files.

"I'm hand delivering these to the US Attorney General, New York's District Attorney, FBI, local police and every reporter who will listen. There must be one honest official left in this country."

CHAPTER VIII

April 19, 2023...

The Justice Department signed the grand jury indictments and issued arrest warrants, Treason for Acts committed during the false-flag terrorist attack of September 11th, 2001. The list read like a who's-who in turn-of-the-century politics. Authorities conducted raids throughout the day and throughout the country...

A pair of FBI agents entered the rebuilt World Trade Center #7, breezed past security and rode a private elevator to the penthouse suite.

They spoke while listening to the Girl from Ipanema as ascending floors lit up on the panel. An FBI agent banged on the elevator wall.

"Hope they constructed this building better than the last one. What did they say collapsed the predecessor?"

The other agent laughed, "Truss failure."

"Truss failure, that's almost as absurd as the Pancake theory."

The elevator dinged, doors parted and the agents walked into the reception area. A sculptured, brass entranceway closed off the interior space.

The receptionist greeted both agents as they walked past her.

"Sirs, you cannot go in there."

She chased after them, they flashed their shields and she sat back down. The FBI agent turned both knobs on the double-doors.

"Locked."

He stepped back a few feet, ran and crashed into the oak panel with his shoulder. He bounced off.

"Pry bar."

The other agent handed him a pry bar, wedged it and pried. Both doors flung open.

The secretary spoke from her desk as they entered, "Be careful, I heard a loud noise in there a few minutes ago."

The FBI agents glanced around at the majestic office, more like a series of offices, each with a perched-view of Manhattan. Various bronze Roman sculptures stood on pedestals in every corner of the space. Original works from the Masters, hung behind glass, down each corridor. The FBI agents searched room-to-room.

"Lucky Larry...Lucky Larry. Your secretary told us you're here."

The FBI agents motioned to each other. One opened the door while the other covered the entranceway.

"Give yourself up. Don't be a fool."

They explored another office then another, then another. They reached the last closed door. They cracked it open into an all-window, overhead view of Ground Zero and spotted a spacious desk with a tall, leather chair behind it, facing away from them. Sun gleamed through a hole in the upper headrest of the seat.

"We're here. It's over. You have the right to remain silent."

The other agent stepped closer to the desk, "Probably should have remained silent years ago. Remember, 'pull it', Larry? Bet you wish you could take back those words. Admission against interest, that's the judicial term, right?"

Both agents approached the chair.

"Turn around Larry. Hope you didn't spend all that insurance money."

"May have to repay it."

The FBI agent grabbed the chair and spun it around as the other trained his gun on the seat. As the chair twirled, a headless body slumped forward and fell to the floor.

"That's the least of his problems."

"Blew his head clean off. Nothing left but a torso with arms and legs sticking out."

"Not so lucky anymore."

They removed and bagged the .45 caliber pistol from his hand and searched the cherry-wood finish desk.

"There's a note."

The FBI agent unfolded the page and read the written message aloud, "I declare my innocence. Myself and my family played no part in the conspiracy of 9/11. I ended my life so that they may live in Peace. I lived through the holocaust only to experience this antisemitic witch hunt which reminds me of the Nazi treatment of the Jews during WW2. I am innocent of the 9/11 crime, signed L.S."

The FBI agent crumpled up the note, lit it on fire and tossed it into the metal wastebasket.

At the same time, inside the Freedom Tower, lower Manhattan, executive suite offices...

Sitting behind a grandiose desk, surrounded by accolades and pictures of himself during 9/11, Gotham's ex-Mayor greeted a pair of FBI agents.

"Can I help you?"

The FBI agent read from his index card, "You have the right to remain silent. Anything you say or do can and will be used against you in a court of law. You have the right to an attorney. If you cannot afford an attorney, one will be appointed to you. Do you understand these rights as they have been read to you?"

"Am I under arrest?"

"Yes."

"For what?"

"Treason, tampering with evidence for your actions before, during and after 9/11."

America's Mayor pointed at framed pictures hanging on walls around the office, "Treason on 9/11. Is this a joke? You cannot arrest me."

They tossed the arrest warrants on the desk, "Grand jury says differently."

The ex-Mayor tapped a photograph on his desk, "I'm a 9/11 hero. I saved lives." He picked up the arrest warrant and perused the charges, "Removing steel, when did that become a crime?"

"Evidence, you tampered with evidence. Removing that steel was a felony."

"FEMA tested it before we disposed of it."

"Save it for the trial, Mr. Mayor."

The ex-Mayor came around from behind his desk and walked to an autographed picture of himself and the President, with cheerleader bullhorn in hand, at Ground Zero.

"New Yorkers love me. Standing ovations greet me in every restaurant."

"This is not a popularity contest, it is a crime."

"They'll never convict. I'm innocent."

The FBI agent pulled a tape recorder from his pocket and hit the play button. 9/11 recordings of countdowns before each of the building collapses filled the room. Voices on the tape instructed the Mayor to vacate World Trade Center building #7.

"That proves nothing."

"We turned the guy who provided these tapes."

"When I worked as DA, we needed stronger evidence than that."

The FBI agent pressed the play button again. Gotham's Mayor heard conversations between himself and the FEMA director conspiring to deny all scientific testing and ordering immediate disposal of the crumbled buildings.

"FEMA instructed me to remove the steel. I followed their orders." He collapsed to his seat, "I followed their orders."

"Of all people, you know better than to use the Nuremberg defense."

The FBI agent read again from the beginning, "Mr. Mayor, you have the right to remain silent..."

"I've been silent too long."

He removed a glossy photograph from the wall depicting him standing on a pile of rubble hugging firefighters and tossed it into a trashcan, "I knew this day would come. Call my wife then call the DA."

In a rural area in Wyoming, authorities waited till nightfall and approached the farmhouse with a detached barn. They knocked on the wooden front door.

No answer.

"Mr. Vice-President, open up."

They pressed the doorbell. Nothing, not even a chime.

An agent pushed his face against the window, "No lights on."

"Break it open."

They took the battering ram and smashed it against the door, splintering it in half.

"We have a warrant for your arrest."

The FBI agents flicked the light switches.

"Electricity's out."

"No, the neighbor's lights are on. Someone blew the fuse."

They turned on flashlights and prowled through the residence.

"Go downstairs, check for the fuse box."

An FBI agent crept through the house while his partner headed downstairs to the fuse box.

In the living room, beneath a stained chandelier, someone spread Tarot cards face-up across the table. An upside-down Hanged Man card lorded over a reversed Ace of Wands, crossed by an upright Five of Swords sandwiched between an Eight of Cups and Four of Swords, all above the Moon card. A Quartet of Tarot cards lined up to the side of the Celtic Cross, from bottom to top, a reversed Two of Wands, upside-down Page of Cups, upright Fool card and a reverse Temperance card ruled above them all. The FBI agent swept the fortunes off the table.

He investigated the rest of the living room then moved on to the kitchen. Fluorescent lights crackled then illuminated black marker wall etchings of Triskele, Triquerta, Awen and a Sun Wheel symbol. A replica baphomet hung on a wire from the ceiling.

"Circuits back on."

"I know I nearly jumped out of my skin. Check out this bizarre shit."

They examined the Pagan symbols.

"Know what any of these mean?"

"No idea."

"Clear the main floor bedrooms, I'll sneak around upstairs."

The FBI agent walked up the spiral staircase and saw coagulating blood streaming down the hall, seeping from beneath the bedroom door. He stood with his back to the wall, reached over and slowly turned the handle. He flung open the door, entered the room and turned on the light switch.

A severed goat's head rested in a stainless steel bowl, overflowing with crimson life. The rest of the goat bled out on the regal, canopy bed, saturating and moistening it. The FBI agent pushed down on the mattress and liquids spilled forth like a squeezed sponge. He ran from the bedroom and hustled downstairs.

"We should get out of here. Call the Crime Scene Unit and we'll wait outside."

"In a minute, follow me."

He brought the agent to an upstairs bathroom and shined his flashlight on the porcelain, claw-footed bathtub. Dead collies with their throat's slit nursed several live puppies. The FBI agents rescued the pups from the tub and released them.

They searched every bedroom, bathroom, closet, loft, kitchen, great room, living room, dining room, sitting room, foyer, hallway, vestibule and anteroom, uncovering black robes, red ties and painted, jeweled skulls.

"Nobody's here. Let's wait outside for forensics."

"Agreed, we'll preserve the crime scene."

"Something like that."

The FBI agent took a last look out the bay window, scanning the backyard and detached barn. He saw a faint flickering light in the barn window.

Both agents raced to the wooden stable door and smashed it open.

"Mr. Vice-President, we have a warrant for your arrest."

The flickering grew lighter and lighter as they climbed a ladder attached to the loft. Haystacks and melting wax candles, strategically placed at every point of an upside-down pentagram, drawn in red chalk across dark-stained wooden floorboards, encircled the Vice President.

Dressed in dark clothing and penny-loafers with a goat-head pendant dangling from his neck, he rested on a coffin-shaped table, both eyes blotted black and arms outstretched.

His wrists were slit to the bone. They dangled from his skin, blood poured through the loft floor and mixed with hay and sawdust below. A snake-curved knife, drenched, leaned on the table leg near his hand.

"Check his pulse."

"Don't bother. There's enough blood here to kill two men."

Candlewicks melted and melted and melted on top of haystacks until they sank through their base and set the barn ablaze. FBI agents rushed out as flames engulfed the barn. The next of Kin failed to claim the charred remains.

Local SWAT, dressed in black military fatigues and FBI officers in green-labeled raincoats, surrounded acres of sprawling ranch in the heart of Crawford, Texas. The Bureau of Alcohol, Tobacco, and Firearms, an agency whose inexplicable jurisdiction covered three legal activities, arrived late in canvas covered army trucks, fortified to the teeth with itchy weapons, poorly written press releases and trailed by gas-inducing modified Abrams tanks.

The gathering force tripped ground sensors, alerting the Secret Service guards inside to form a pre-positioned, two-tiered, uzi-armed defensive circle around the mansion.

A good ole' American Constitutional standoff, replete with guns, ensued.

To this day, nobody knows who fired first but everyone knows who fired last. SWAT, BATF and FBI wiped out the detail and swarmed the house by climbing up ladders, landing on rooftops, repelling down walls, smashing through windows and breaking down doors. They haphazardly tossed in CO2 gas, flash-bang grenades, tear gas and incendiary devices.

In moments, fires raged across the compound. Emergency water sprinklers, aided by regional fire departments, tempered down the flames.

Authorities ransacked the residence. Running room to room, throwing people on floors, tasering anything that moved including dogs, cats and a hamster. One agency starting shooting causing a chain-reaction of violence. Bullets flew all over the house as PNACs, Neo-cons, Zionists, Bilderbergs and Illuminati ducked for cover.

The former President, quicker on his real feet than on his proverbial feet, dashed for a trap-door exit. He opened the bolted portal and froze, greeted by a mixed quartet of BATF and FBI agents.

They encircled the decider, in pairs, with weapons fixated.

"Stop right there, Mr. President."

The FBI agent handed him a copy of the indictments.

"You are under arrest for the crime of Treason. You have the right to remain silent. You have the right to an attorney. If you cannot afford one..."

"I know my rights and I can afford one."

"Please place your hands behind your..."

The FBI agent caught a bullet through his throat before he finished the sentence. Pair of BATF officers opened fire and downed the FBI agents.

"We'll take it from here, Mr President."

They dragged the FBI agents into another room and staged the bodies.

"Good luck, Mr. President."

The former President escaped into the night, never brought to justice, never seen again.

The SWAT team cleaned out the house and handcuffed members of the PNAC crew, defense contractors and associated CFR members. The SWAT team perp-walked the adults and helped firefighters carry a few younger children to waiting ambulances.

Detective Nash removed his bullet-proof vest and SWAT insignias.

"You saw your raid. I fulfilled my end of the bargain."

Jason removed his green jacket, "You're a man of your word."

Detective Nash and Jason shook hands.

"Hopefully, we don't cross paths again."

"I'm leaving the US for good. Too much trouble here these days. Not like the old days when we ran this country."

Detective Nash held up his index finger, "One week to board a plane. Stay any longer and I'm hunting you down."

"I understand. You know, you'll miss us when we're gone. You will not like the group who will fill the void."

"You not part of that group anymore. You sealed your fate. So I grant you a one-time free pass on that clone business."

Jason winked, "Consider us distant strangers."

"Good. Too bad we missed the big fish today."

"He's always been lucky."

SWAT team members paraded the accused past the entire squad while they drank coffee, smoked cigarettes and regaled one another with their heroic deeds of the day. Detective Nash and Jason Schwartz watched as firefighters carried children out of the compound.

Jason's eye caught the eye of a sole child being cradled by a firefighter. He couldn't be sure. He walked closer to the infant. Goose-bumps popped up through his skin, every hair on his body stood at attention as though saluting a powerful leader, his face reddened then drained, his eyes failed to blink and both arms trembled. He caught himself from falling by balancing on a wooden fence post. He remembered the training and mentally forced himself to breath.

His memory flashed to his youth in synagogue and the Rabbi he admired, using science to poke holes in the myth of the resurrection. He stumbled again.

Detective Nash steadied him and asked, "You, okay?"

"Yeah, yeah, I'll be seeing you."

Jason regained his balance and drifted toward the parking lot. Detective Nash followed.

"Where you going?"

"I just gotta go."

"Leave tomorrow, rejoice today. 9/11's been avenged. This was nothing short of a miracle."

Just as he mouthed the word 'miracle', the same firefighter walked by, carrying the child. Detective Nash gazed into the baby's deep green eyes, lightly touched the long dark hair and clenched his small hand. He stopped in his tracks and watched as a firefighter carried the infant away.

"It's him. I told you today was a miracle, even baby Jesus showed up."

Jason hurried toward the parking lot followed by the detective.

"What's the rush?"

Detective Nash stopped chasing him and stood frozen. He reached into his back pocket and retrieved the coded note.

Celebrate America's Independence at the beginning of every month, until Christmas.
Along the many highway lanes on the Island of New York.
Kicked over the moneychangers tables,
Call him the Dayton Dry Goods Company's heir

Piece-by-piece the answers came to him.

Celebrate America's Independence at the beginning of every month, until Christmas.

America's Independence, the Fourth of July. Beginning of the word, the first letter, July, the letter "J", the next month August, the letter "A", then September, "S", October, "O", November, "N", spelled JASON. The first part, *Jason*, his friend, Jason Schwartz.

Along the many highway lanes on the Island of New York.

Not Staten Island, not Manhattan Island. Long Island, must be Long Island. Many lanes of the Long Island Expressway known by the residents as the L.I.E.. Many lanes, plural, LIEs. Lies. *Jason Lies.*

Kicked over the moneychangers tables,

Easy, that's *Jesus*. He stared at the note as Jason jumped in the car and started the engine.

Call him the Dayton Dry Goods Company's heir.

Call him, Call Jesus. *Call Jesus the Dayton Dry Goods Company Heir*, what does that mean? Dayton Dry Goods Company, he Googled ® it in his cell phone. The response caused him to drop the device. Written across the phone, his answer, Dayton Dry Goods Company eventually evolved into the mega-store 'Target'. He solved the riddle too late, *Jason Lies, Jesus is the Target.*

Detective Nash sprinted to the car. He yelled through the window, "You never wanted to kill the Hitler clone. The Jesus clone, that's who you wanted the whole time. It was always Baby Jesus."

Jason involuntarily yelled back through the driver's side glass. Detective Nash couldn't be certain but he thought he heard him say, "That's the problem. Three days ago...Three days ago...I killed him."

EPILOGUE

The US government arrested and convicted scores of traitors for treason on 9/11. On his last day as Commander-in-Chief, President Jack Fremont III pardoned every one of them.

In Sports news, the Hall of Fame in Cooperstown, New York inducted Jose Canseco for saving baseball.

BlackJack Jones survived the shooting, crawled out of the house and recuperated for months. Under his new cover, he joined a political advisory group and guided a young, ambitious, conservative Mexican-American politician through fund-raising, back-slapping and hypnotic-inducing speech making in a bid to elect the first South of the Border President of the United States.

In Astronomy News, Pluto returned to planet-hood and My Very Educated Mother Just Served Us Nine...Pizzas.

Mossad agent Jason Schwartz rejoined his friends and orchestrated many more false-flag attacks, for sport, on Palestinians.

In Death Penalty News, the government of the United States of America hung Ben Bernanke for violating the Coinage Act of 1792.

Child Protective Services seized Infant Jesus and crucified him through the foster care system. An unmarried woman from Bethlehem, Pennsylvania adopted the infant and raised him as a Muslim.

In Medical and Ironic News, former Environmental Protection Agency head Christie Todd Whitman died from lung cancer after ingesting toxic fumes at Ground Zero.

General Barker, deemed courageous by the mainstream media for using a nuke, toured the speaking circuit and whipped up the next generation as cannon fodder for future imperialistic military adventures.

The US Congress amended the Constitution, adding a 28th Amendment outlawing the killing of clones and granted them voting rights of 3/5ths of a person.

Detective Nash pounded on the door and yelled from the front porch, "This is the police, come out with your hands up."

Dr. Abrams peeked through a cracked-open shade. He spotted Detective Nash and a pair of police officers, one gesturing the other, silently, to walk around to the back of the house.

"You're surrounded. Allow us in to examine that clone. Surrender yourselves peacefully and avoid arrest."

He shouted loudly from inside the house, "You're not taking him from me."

Dr. Abrams scooped up Baby Hitler and headed to the basement. Baby Hitler screamed bloody murder.

Detective Nash kicked in the front door, simultaneously as the other officers smashed through the back door. They all met in the living room.

"Be careful, consider him armed."

Room-by-room, they kicked open doors and cleared them.

"Main floor, clean."

The police officer nodded to the basement. Tired of kicking open doors, Detective Nash merely opened this one by turning the knob. A police officer's gun peered around the corner.

"We know you're down there."

The other cop rolled across the opening, to the opposite side and drew his weapon.

"Allow us to examine him and investigate the care that you provided."

Dr. Abrams yelled upstairs, "We're not going anywhere. You stole my other son."

"Nobody stole him. We needed to investigate how he ended up in the middle of a shoot-out in Texas."

Baby Hitler whimpered. Dr. Abrams jammed a pacifier into the infant's mouth.

"I don't know how he ended up there. He was missing for a few days. I reported him missing."

"Exactly, so we investigated. Just like now."

Dr. Abrams inched toward showing himself from behind the crates, "You never returned him."

Police officers crept down the stairwell, trailed by Detective Nash, checking both sides of the basement as they descended.

"We will return him. He checked out in fine physical shape."

Dr. Abrams squeezed Baby Hitler tighter as he lowered him to the ground. Baby Hitler groaned.

"Don't put that child in jeopardy."

"Stay away."

"Consider the best interest of the child and allow us to examine him."

Dr. Abrams crouched lower, "What kind of examination will you conduct?"

"Health, reflexes, weight, height, and a small blood sample."

Dr. Abrams clutched the infant beneath him, behind stacked packages. He watched between cardboard boxes as both officers and the detective navigated through the maze of files cabinets, medical equipment and boxes of papers.

"You're going to kill him because he's a clone."

Detective Nash stood ahead of the officers, "I promise not to harm him. Congress changed the laws, granting clones equal rights to people."

Baby Hitler screamed and cried. Dr. Abrams muffled him again.

"You tried to steal him from me before."

The police officer covered the area and motioned to the other officer to approach a region full of cardboard boxes.

"Okay, we're backing off. No need for confrontation."

Baby Hitler yelled again. The police officer pointed with his gun directly at the box.

"You win. We're leaving."

Detective Nash motioned the officer's back. He opened both sides of his shirt.

"Unarmed, see for yourself."

Dr. Abrams peeked above the boxes, "Very brave, last time we met, I told you I'd kill you."

"I've come to know you. I know I can reason with you."

"He's all I have left."

"Right after the exam, I'll personally return him."

Baby Hitler squirmed around, causing Dr. Abrams to grip him tighter, "Swear to me no harm comes to him."

"Scout's honor."

Dr. Abrams lifted his head above the crate, and lowered the cocked gun as Baby Hitler yanked on his arm.

"And you'll return him, right after?"

"Immediately."

"Alright, I'm coming out."

Dr. Abrams stood up, carrying Baby Hitler, from behind the boxes. Baby Hitler squirmed and jerked on his arm harder, causing him to drop the gun. The handgun slammed on to the cement floor and fired.

Detective Nash fell back clutching his chin.

The other officers jumped behind metal bookcases and fired at Dr.Abrams as he grabbed Baby Hitler and ducked back behind a box. Each bullet missed, leaving Swiss Cheese holes in the cardboard.

Detective Nash yelled in a disjointed voice from his contorted face, "He blew off my mouth. I'm dying. Help me."

Detective Nash passed out and never awoke from this coma.

The other officers hid behind a heavy metal cabinet and called for back-up.

The police officers reloaded, "You're fucking dead now. You'll be hunted down by every cop in America."

"It was an accident. The gun slipped."

"Kill a law enforcement agent and you receive the cop death penalty. No trial for you."

The police officers fired wildly, bouncing bullets off steel metal cabinets, shooting through walls and ricocheting shots down stairs as they traced backwards out of the basement.

Dr. Abrams returned unaimed fire and escaped through a ground level hatch into the garage. He jumped into his SUV and peeled out of the driveway.

The police officers rushed back into the house and tended to their mortally wounded 'thin-blue-line' friend. Law Enforcement officers from all precincts, retired cops, detectives, desk patrolmen, junior league officers, paper pushers, disability kings and flatfoots dropped their civilian cases, ignored all public emergencies and hunted down the killer of their own. Nobody killed a cop and got away with it.

Nobody.

They re-routed helicopters from emergency calls, sped away from life-threatening car accidents, stopped looking for missing children, ended street patrols, halted mid-TASER on a handicapped veteran, ceased shoving bicyclists, discontinued writing 'Assault on Officer' summons for every instance of their brutality and loaded their weapons for killing.

Dr. Abrams drove all night...or several nights...or weeks. Everything blurred together. Saving his remaining son dominated the brief remainder of his life. Child Protective Services stole Infant Jesus after the raid and gave him away. Local police labeled Dr. Abrams a 'person-of-interest' for the unresolved shooting death of his son, Toddler Lincoln. Time plotted against him. Eventually, either death or the law catches up to us all.

Nobody was left. They conspired to undermine his dream of saving America from itself. His own government tried to kill him.

Was America worth saving at all?

Maybe he should give up, hand over his last son to the bureaucrats and end his life. That's the easy way out, the coward's way out. America must be deserving of redemption. Honorable citizens inhabit the place. Revolutionary blood flows in their veins. Vampires in the government, bloodsuckers in the banks and leeches in foreign countries cannot drain every rebellious drop.

One man can make a difference. If he cannot, then his son can.

Dr. Abrams stopped and idled the SUV at the cul-de-sac curb of a sprawling estate. He jimmied open the sturdy wrought iron gates with a crowbar, returned to the car and opened the rear passenger door. Dr. Abrams unlocked the car seat, grabbed the bundled, sedated infant and hustled up the stone-paved walkway.

He brushed dirt from the blue slate porch with his free hand and gently laid down the bassinet. He wiped down the sides with a cloth, tucked in a plush baby blue blanket, kissed him on the forehead and popped a pacifier into the his mouth.

"Good luck, little Adolf. Be good for your new parents. They will take care of you, nurture you and teach you. I love you, son."

He rang the doorbell and hurried back down the driveway, passing back through the gate with brass house number '322' welded artistically into the wrought iron bars.

As he turned around to speed away, both headlights of the SUV crossed over the front yard, revealing the surname of Baby Hitler's new parents, stenciled in wooden letters, spelled out across both sides of the mailbox.

'R-o-t-h-s-c-h-i-l-d.'

THE END